POKÉMON™

BLACK AND WHITE

VOL.9

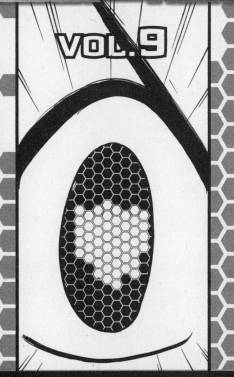

Story by **HIDENORI KUSAKA**
Art by **SATOSHI YAMAMOTO**

Pokémon Black and White
Volume 9
VIZ Kids Edition

Story by HIDENORI KUSAKA
Art by SATOSHI YAMAMOTO

© 2013 Pokémon.
© 1995-2013 Nintendo/Creatures Inc./GAME FREAK inc.
TM and ® and character names are trademarks of Nintendo.
POCKET MONSTER SPECIAL (Magazine Edition)
by Hidenori KUSAKA, Satoshi YAMAMOTO
© 1997 Hidenori KUSAKA, Satoshi YAMAMOTO
All rights reserved.
Original Japanese edition published by SHOGAKUKAN.
English translation rights in the United States of America and Canada
arranged with SHOGAKUKAN.

English Adaptation / Bryant Turnage
Translation / Tetsuichiro Miyaki
Touch-up & Lettering / Susan Daigle-Leach
Design / Fawn Lau
Editor / Annette Roman

Printed in the U.S.A.

Published by VIZ Media, LLC
P.O. Box 77010
San Francisco, CA 94107

10 9 8 7 6 5 4 3 2 1
First printing, April 2013

www.vizkids.com

www.viz.com

POKÉMON

BLACK and WHITE

VOL.9

THE STORY THUS FAR!

Pokémon Trainer Black is exploring the mysterious Unova region with his brand-new Pokédex. Pokémon Trainer White runs a thriving talent agency for performing Pokémon. While traveling together, their paths cross with Team Plasma, a nefarious group that advocates releasing your Pokémon into the wild! Now Black and White are off on their own separate journeys of discovery...

BLACK'S dream is to win the Pokémon League!

WHITE'S dream is to make her Tepig Gigi a star!

Black's Munna, MUSHA, helps him think clearly by temporarily "eating" his dream.

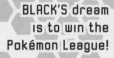

White's Tepig, GIGI, and Black's Pignite, NITE, get along like peanut butter and jelly! But now Gigi has left White for another Trainer...

Adventure 29
Drawing Bridges

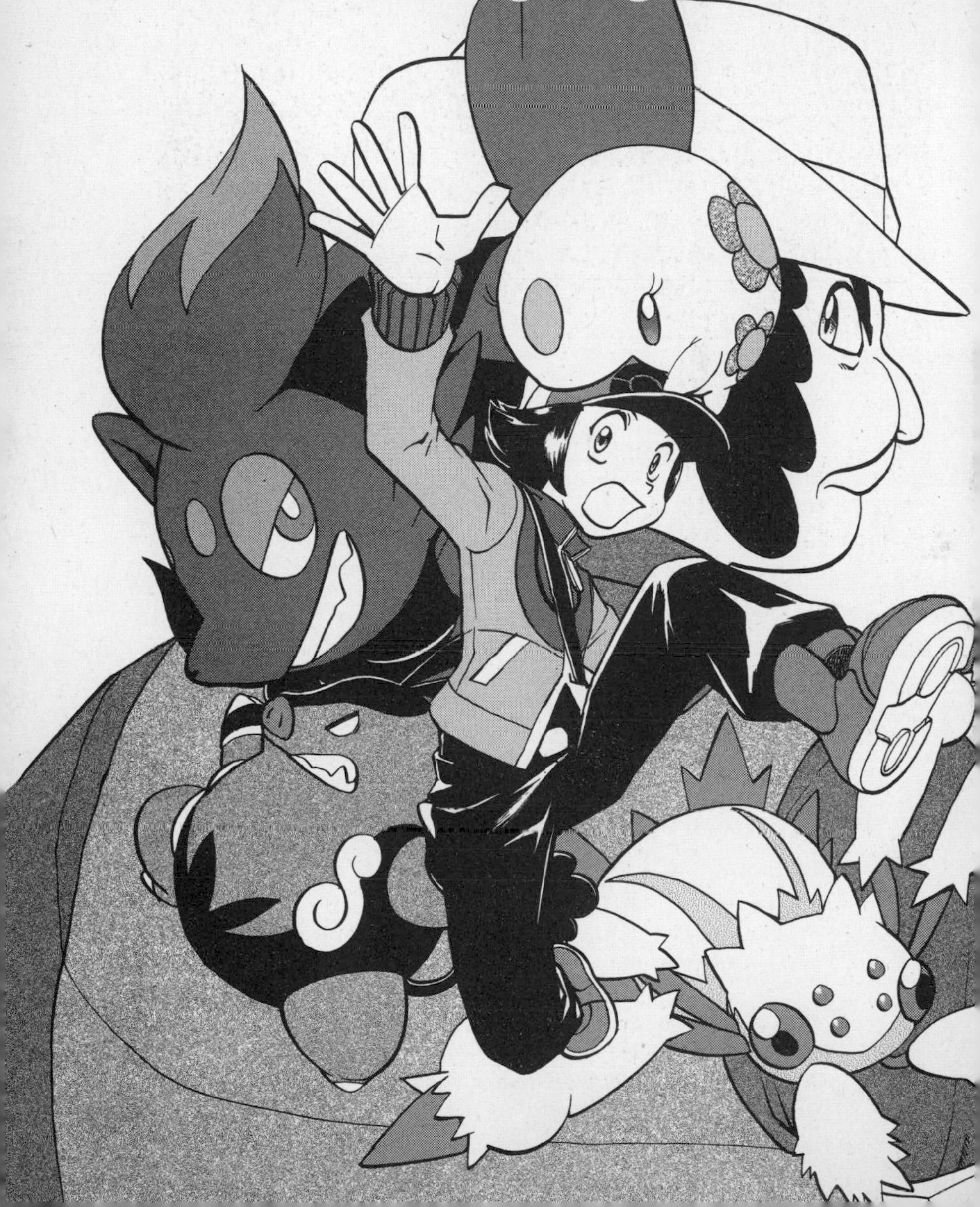

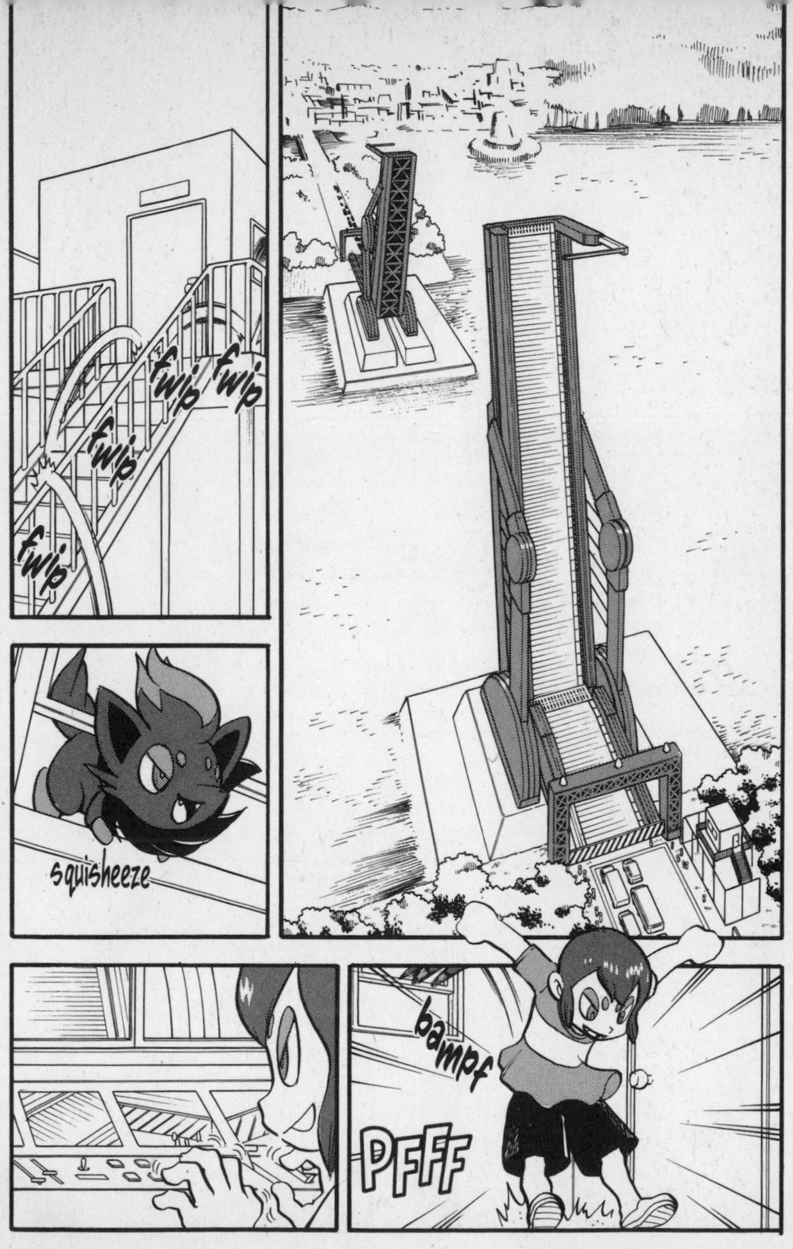
fwip
fwip
fwip
fwip
squisheeze
bampf
PFFF

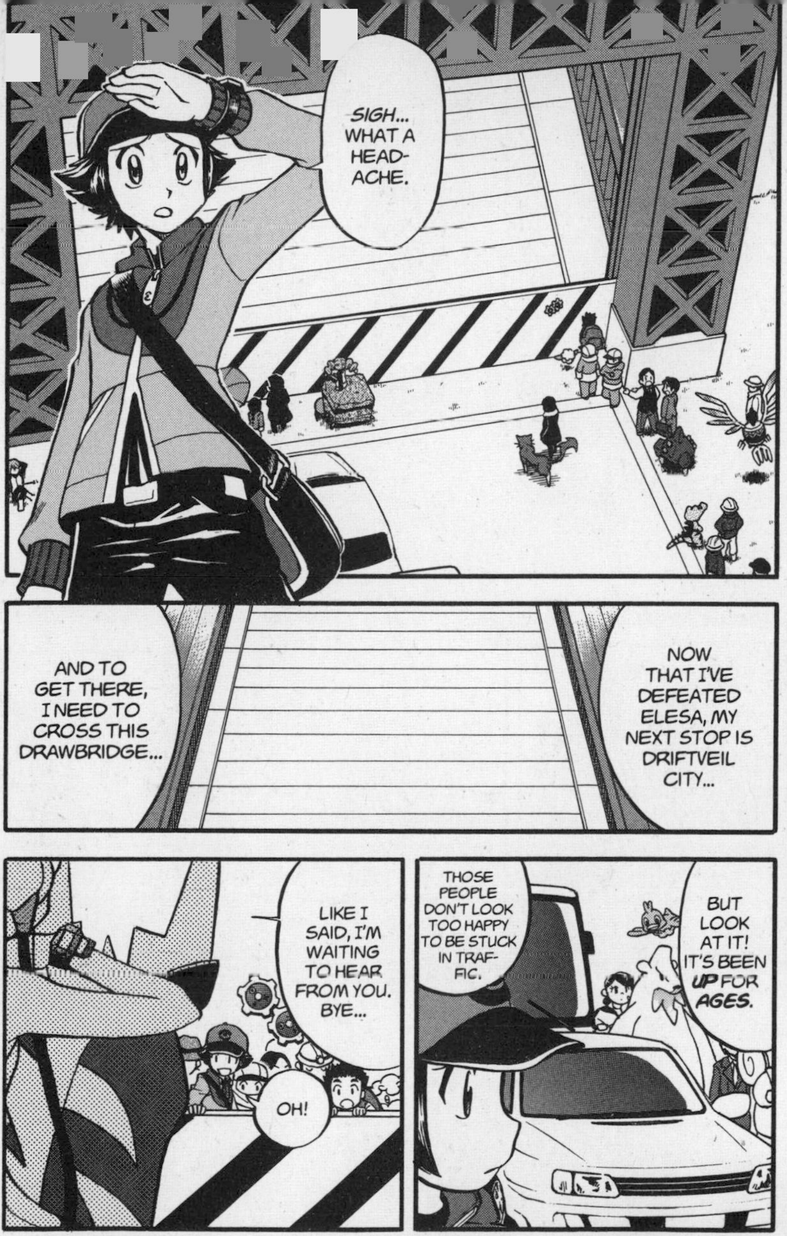
SIGH... WHAT A HEAD-ACHE.
NOW THAT I'VE DEFEATED ELESA, MY NEXT STOP IS DRIFTVEIL CITY...
AND TO GET THERE, I NEED TO CROSS THIS DRAWBRIDGE...
BUT LOOK AT IT! IT'S BEEN *UP* FOR *AGES.*
THOSE PEOPLE DON'T LOOK TOO HAPPY TO BE STUCK IN TRAF-FIC.
LIKE I SAID, I'M WAITING TO HEAR FROM YOU. BYE...
OH!

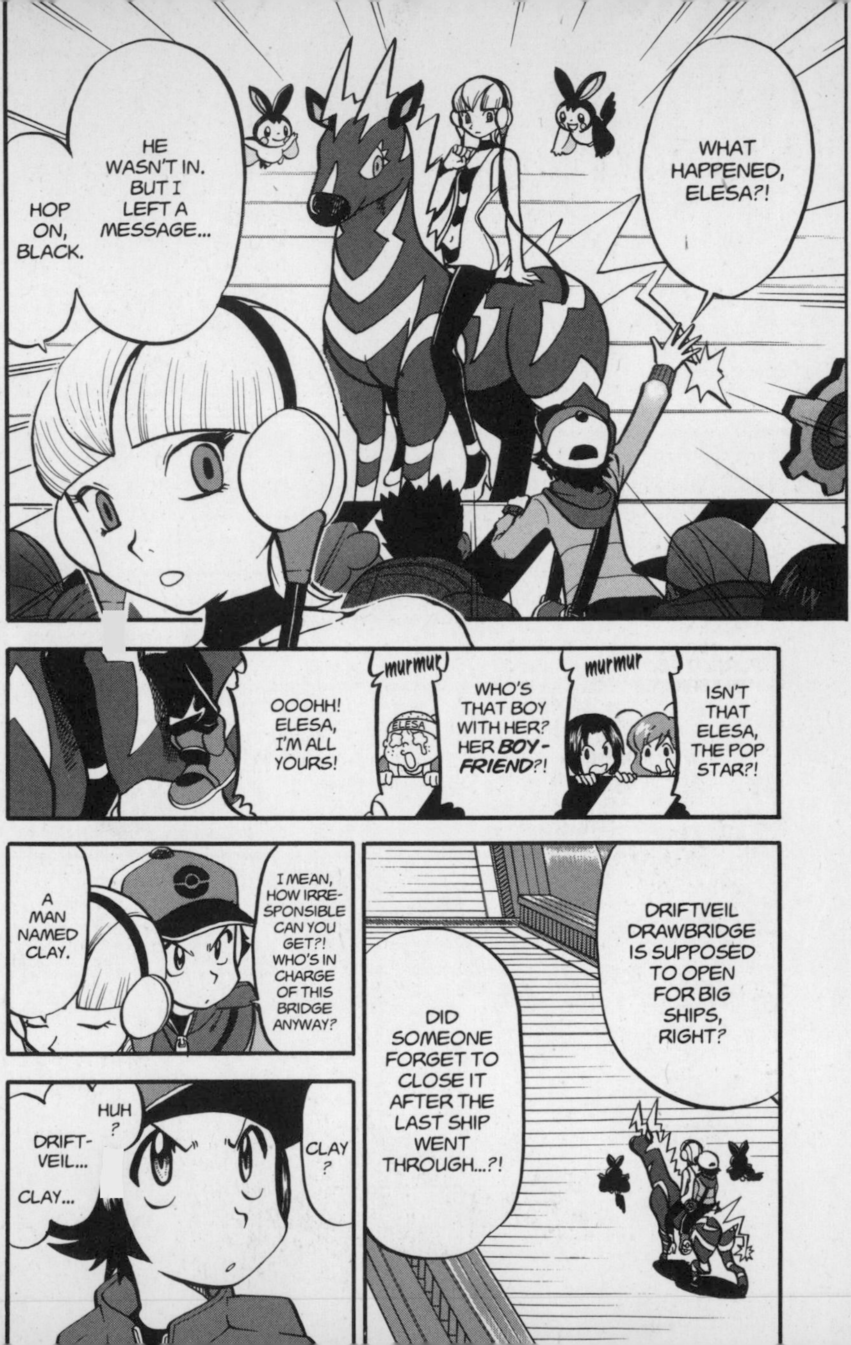
WHAT HAPPENED, ELESA?!
HE WASN'T IN. BUT I LEFT A MESSAGE...
HOP ON, BLACK.
ISN'T THAT ELESA, THE POP STAR?!
murmur
WHO'S THAT BOY WITH HER? HER BOY-FRIEND?!
murmur
ELESA
OOOHH! ELESA, I'M ALL YOURS!
DRIFTVEIL DRAWBRIDGE IS SUPPOSED TO OPEN FOR BIG SHIPS, RIGHT?
DID SOMEONE FORGET TO CLOSE IT AFTER THE LAST SHIP WENT THROUGH...?!
I MEAN, HOW IRRESPONSIBLE CAN YOU GET?! WHO'S IN CHARGE OF THIS BRIDGE ANYWAY?
A MAN NAMED CLAY.
CLAY?
HUH?
DRIFT-VEIL...
CLAY...

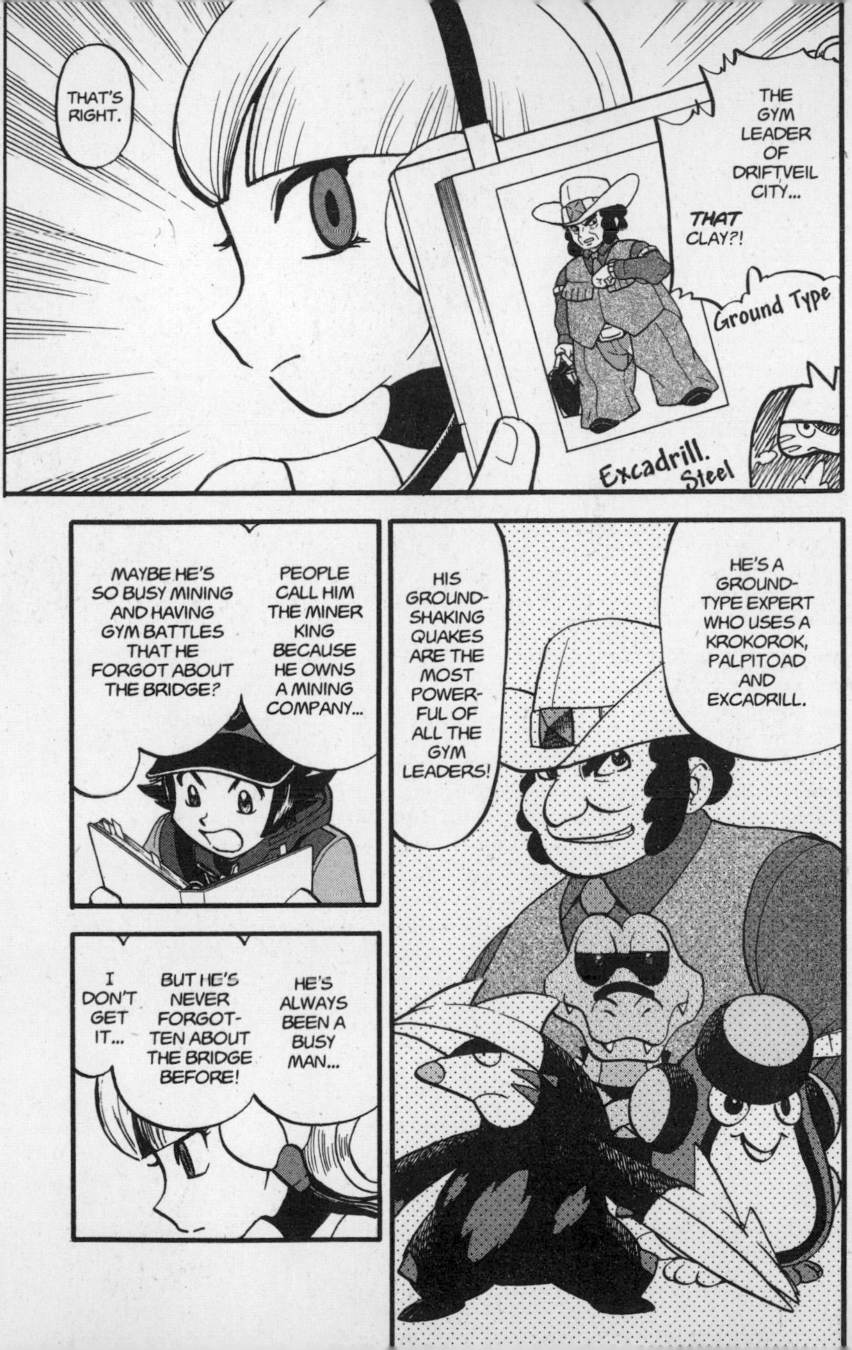

THE GYM LEADER OF DRIFTVEIL CITY...
THAT CLAY?!
THAT'S RIGHT.
Ground Type
Excadrill. Steel
HE'S A GROUND-TYPE EXPERT WHO USES A KROKOROK, PALPITOAD AND EXCADRILL.
HIS GROUND-SHAKING QUAKES ARE THE MOST POWERFUL OF ALL THE GYM LEADERS!
PEOPLE CALL HIM THE MINER KING BECAUSE HE OWNS A MINING COMPANY...
MAYBE HE'S SO BUSY MINING AND HAVING GYM BATTLES THAT HE FORGOT ABOUT THE BRIDGE?
HE'S ALWAYS BEEN A BUSY MAN...
BUT HE'S NEVER FORGOTTEN ABOUT THE BRIDGE BEFORE!
I DON'T GET IT...

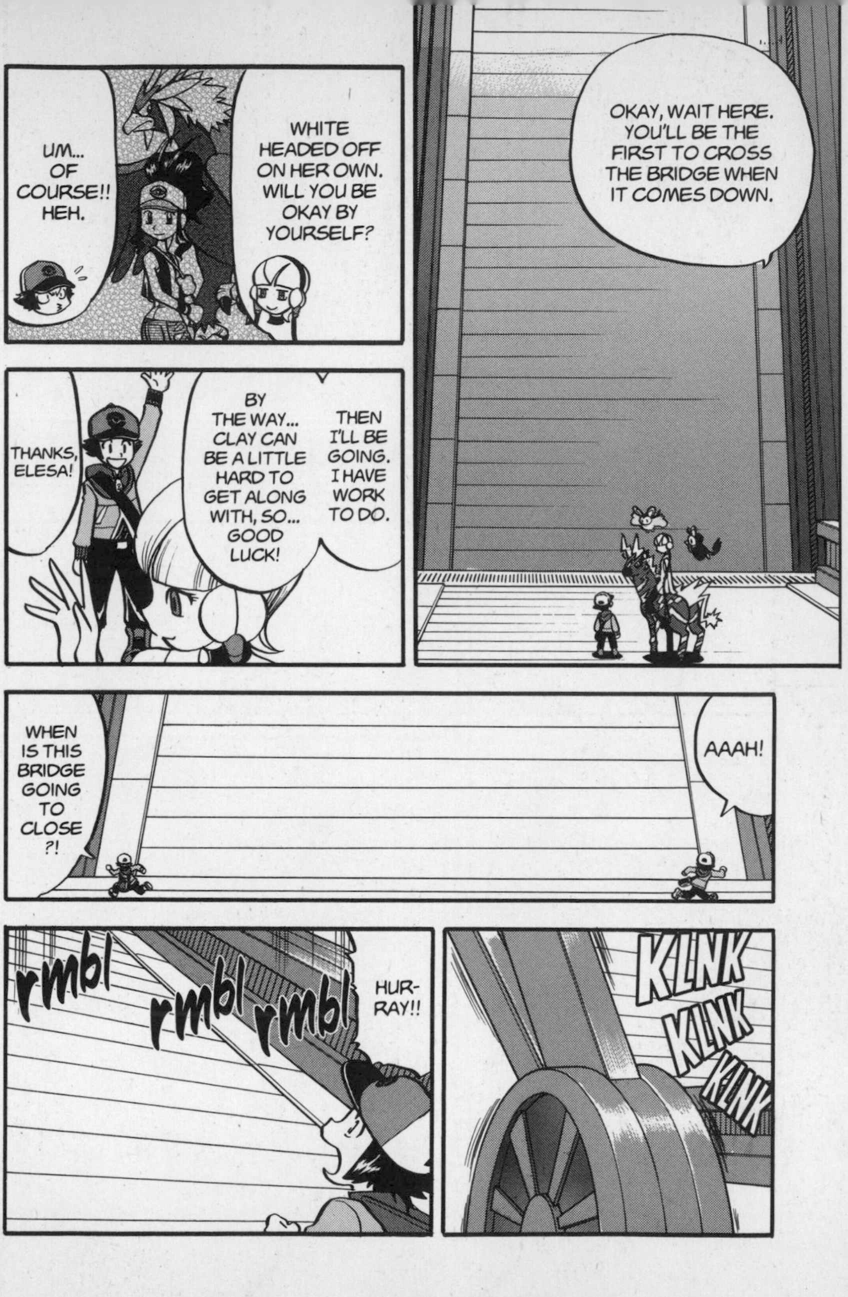

OKAY, WAIT HERE. YOU'LL BE THE FIRST TO CROSS THE BRIDGE WHEN IT COMES DOWN.
WHITE HEADED OFF ON HER OWN. WILL YOU BE OKAY BY YOURSELF?
UM... OF COURSE!! HEH.
BY THE WAY... CLAY CAN BE A LITTLE HARD TO GET ALONG WITH, SO... GOOD LUCK!
THEN I'LL BE GOING. I HAVE WORK TO DO.
THANKS, ELESA!
WHEN IS THIS BRIDGE GOING TO CLOSE ?!
AAAH!
rmbl rmbl rmbl
HUR-RAY!!
KLNK KLNK KLNK

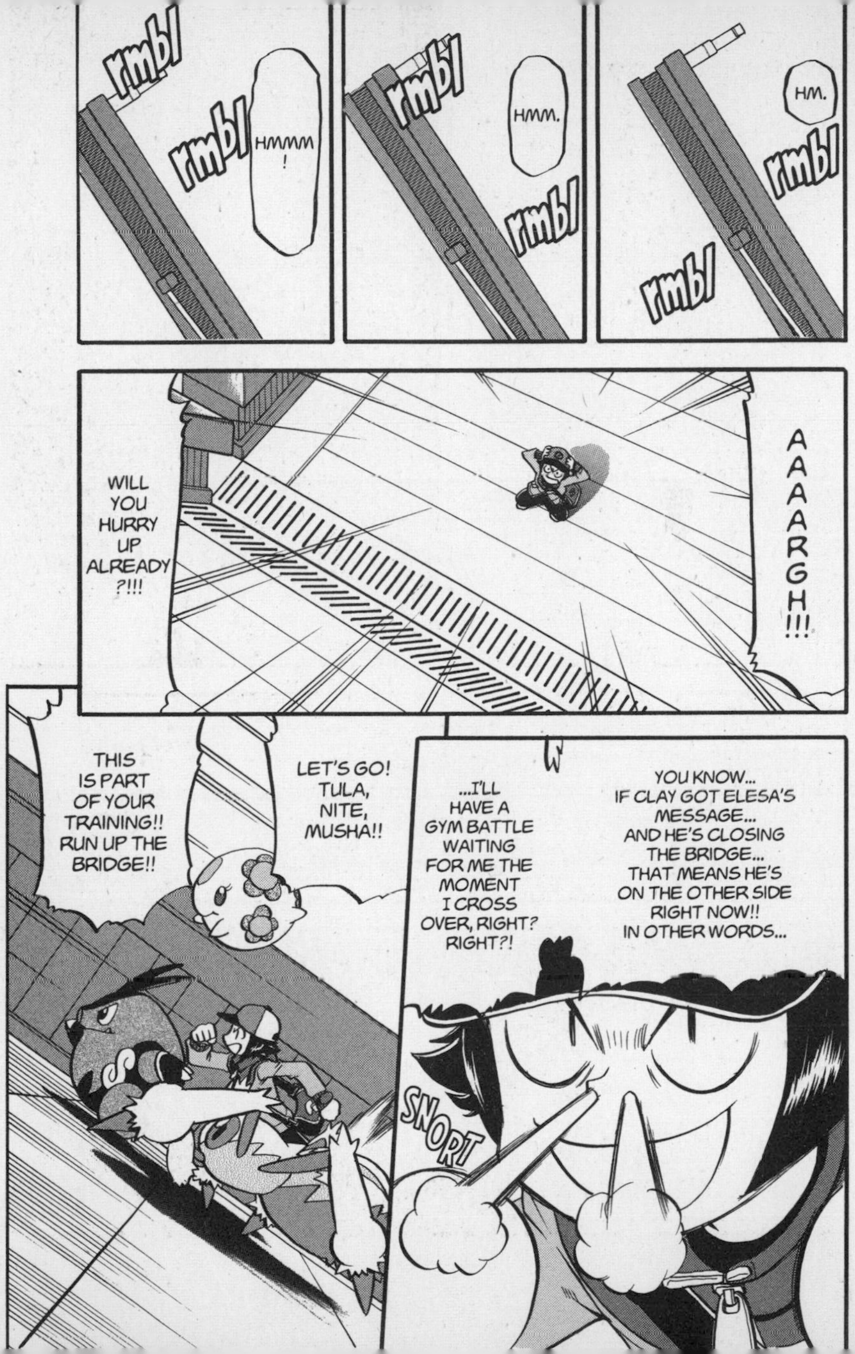
rmbl
rmbl
HMMM!
rmbl
rmbl
HMM.
rmbl
rmbl
HM.
WILL YOU HURRY UP ALREADY?!!!
AAAARGH!!!
THIS IS PART OF YOUR TRAINING!! RUN UP THE BRIDGE!!
LET'S GO! TULA, NITE, MUSHA!!
...I'LL HAVE A GYM BATTLE WAITING FOR ME THE MOMENT I CROSS OVER, RIGHT? RIGHT?!
YOU KNOW... IF CLAY GOT ELESA'S MESSAGE... AND HE'S CLOSING THE BRIDGE... THAT MEANS HE'S ON THE OTHER SIDE RIGHT NOW!! IN OTHER WORDS...
SNORT

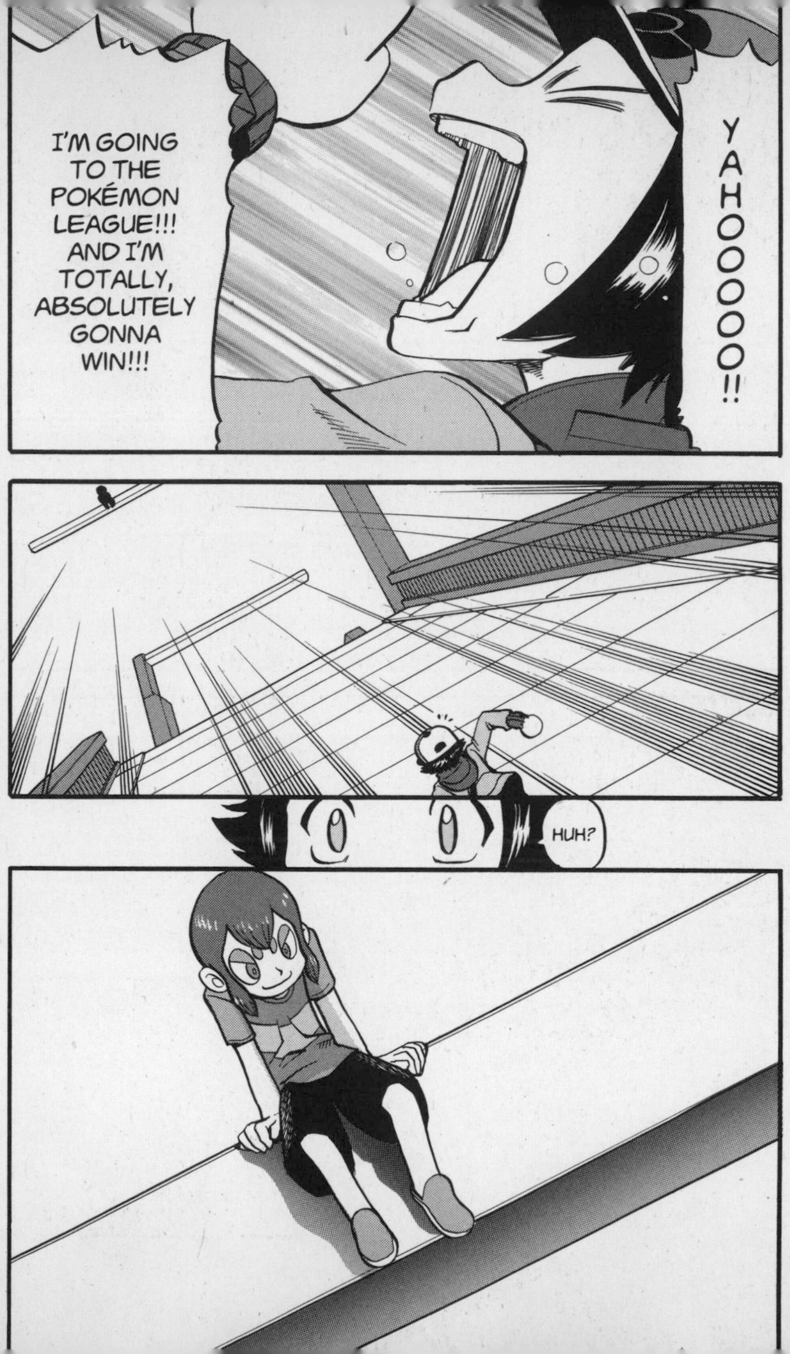
YAHOOOOOO!!
I'M GOING TO THE POKÉMON LEAGUE!!! AND I'M TOTALLY, ABSOLUTELY GONNA WIN!!!
HUH?

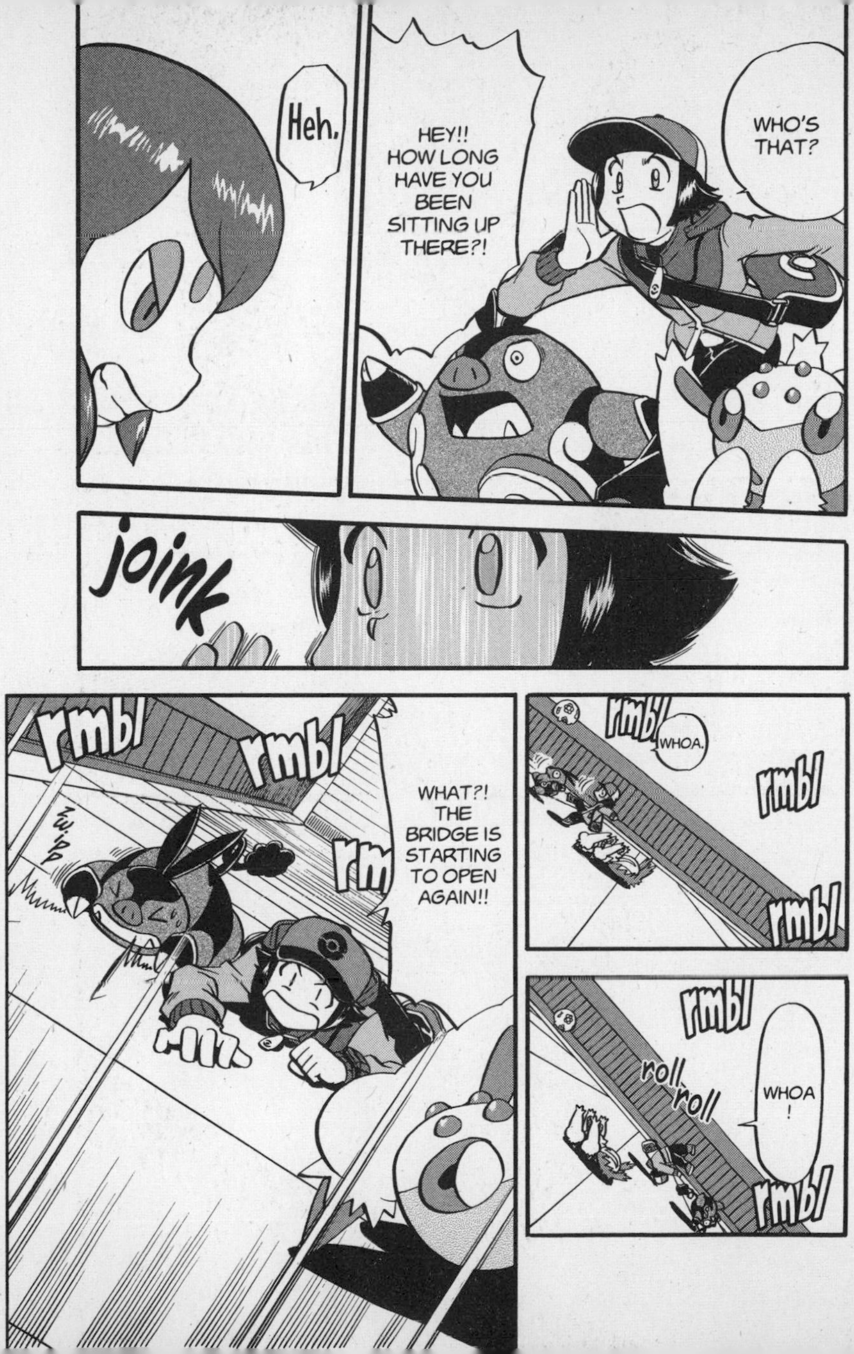
Heh.
HEY!! HOW LONG HAVE YOU BEEN SITTING UP THERE?!
WHO'S THAT?
joink
rmbl
rmbl
rm
WHAT?! THE BRIDGE IS STARTING TO OPEN AGAIN!!
rmbl
WHOA.
rmbl
rmbl
rmbl
roll roll
WHOA!
rmbl

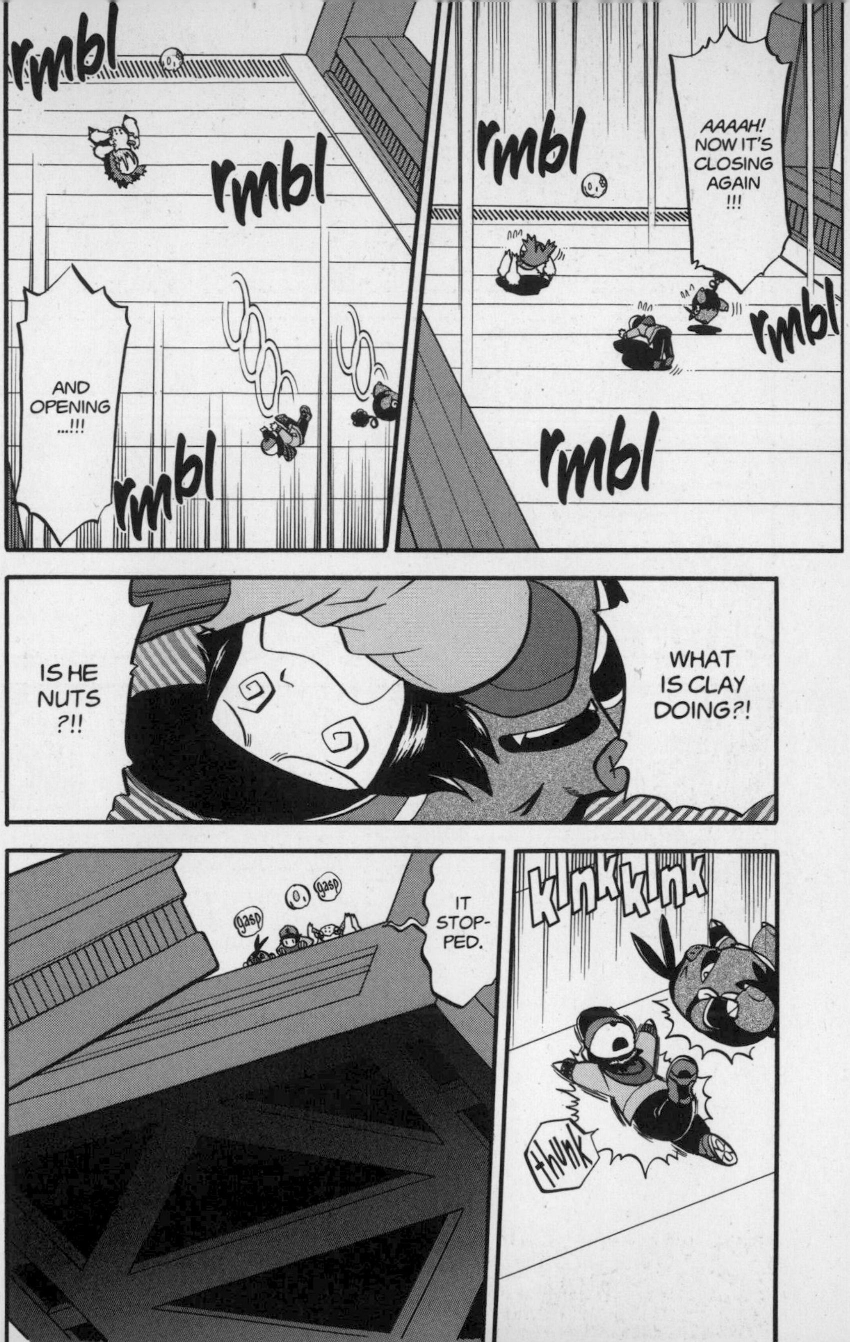
rmbl
rmbl
AND OPENING ...!!!
rmbl
rmbl
AAAAH! NOW IT'S CLOSING AGAIN !!!
rmbl
rmbl
IS HE NUTS ?!!
WHAT IS CLAY DOING?!
gasp
gasp
IT STOP-PED.
klinkklink
thunk

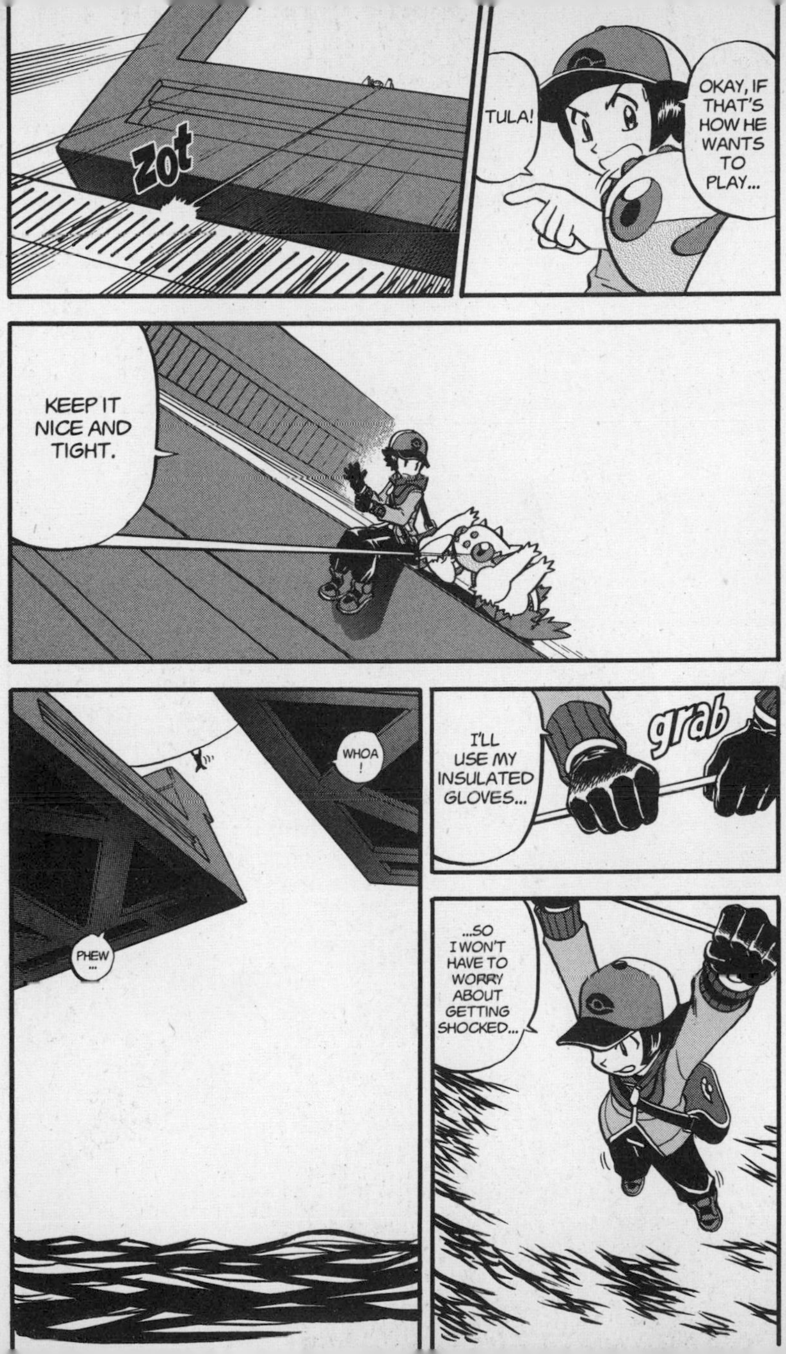
Zot
OKAY, IF THAT'S HOW HE WANTS TO PLAY...
TULA!
KEEP IT NICE AND TIGHT.
grab
I'LL USE MY INSULATED GLOVES...
WHOA!
PHEW...
...SO I WON'T HAVE TO WORRY ABOUT GETTING SHOCKED...

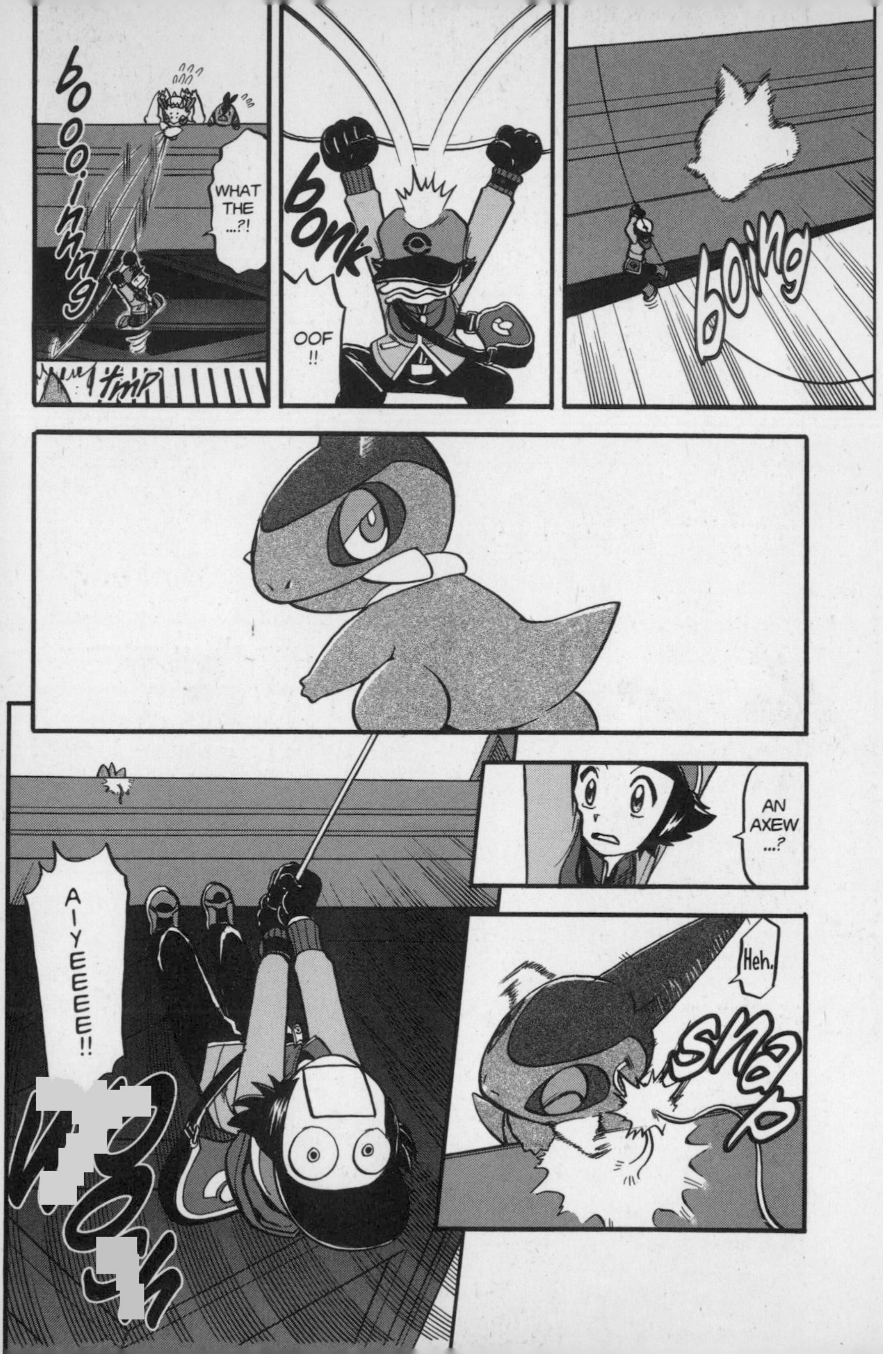
booo.innng
WHAT THE ...?!
tmp
bonk
OOF !!
boing
AN AXEW ...?
AIYEEEEE!!
Heh.
snap

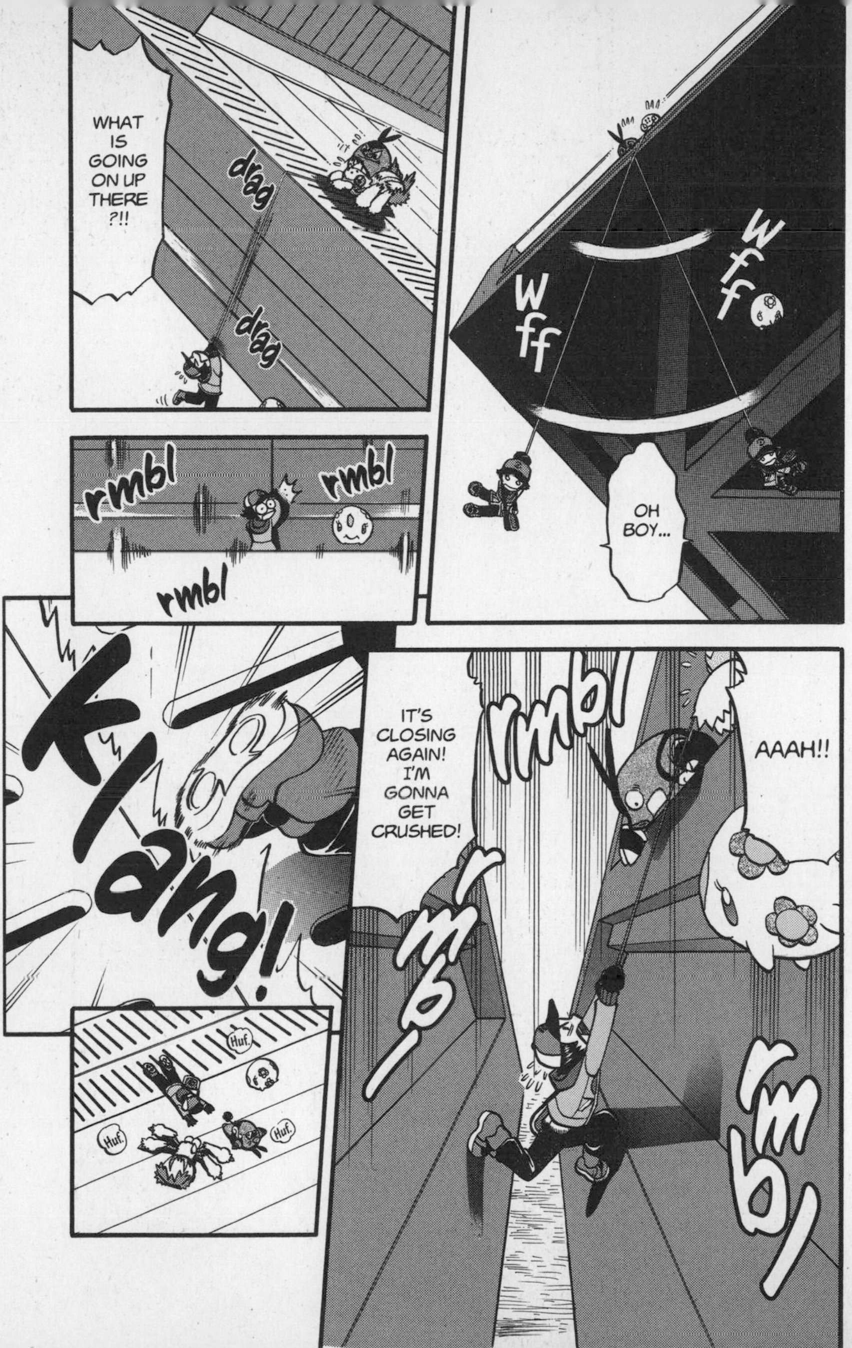
WHAT IS GOING ON UP THERE ?!!
drag
drag
wff
wff
OH BOY...
rmbl
rmbl
rmbl
klang!
Huf.
Huf.
Huf.
rmbl
IT'S CLOSING AGAIN! I'M GONNA GET CRUSHED!
AAAH!!
rmbl
rmbl

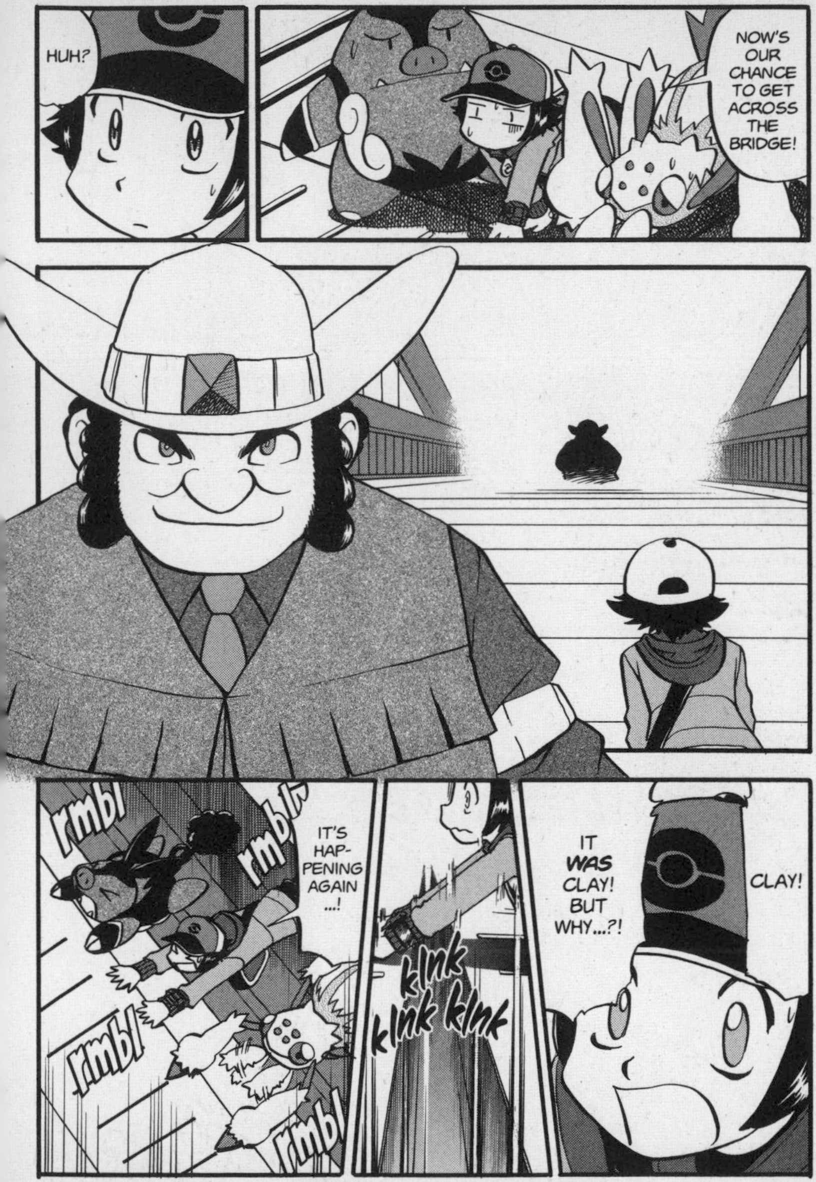
HUH?
NOW'S OUR CHANCE TO GET ACROSS THE BRIDGE!
rmbl
rmbl
rmbl
rmbl
IT'S HAP-PENING AGAIN ...!
klink klink klink
IT WAS CLAY! BUT WHY...?!
CLAY!

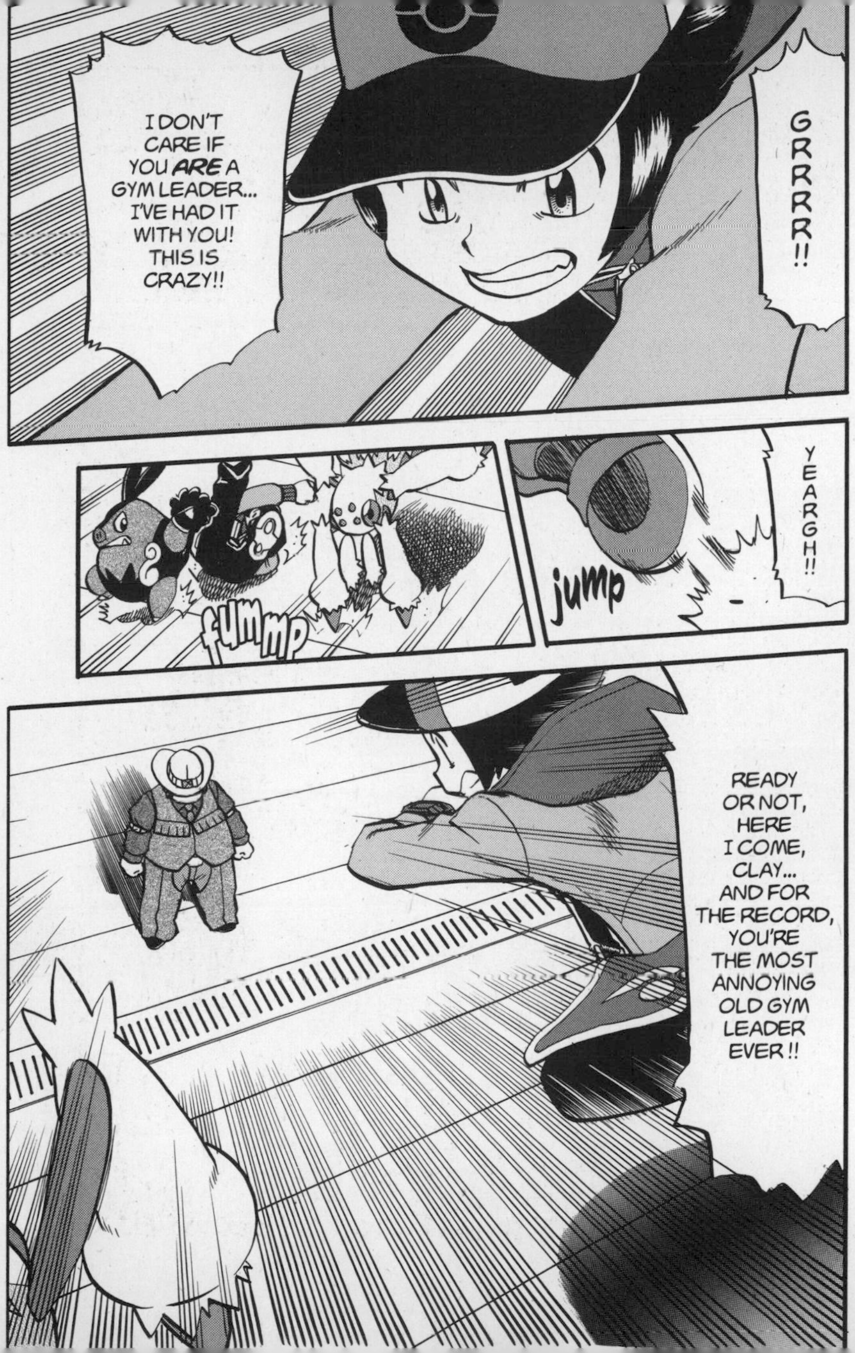
I DON'T CARE IF YOU ARE A GYM LEADER... I'VE HAD IT WITH YOU! THIS IS CRAZY!!
GRRRR!!
YEARGH!!
jump
fummp
READY OR NOT, HERE I COME, CLAY... AND FOR THE RECORD, YOU'RE THE MOST ANNOYING OLD GYM LEADER EVER!!

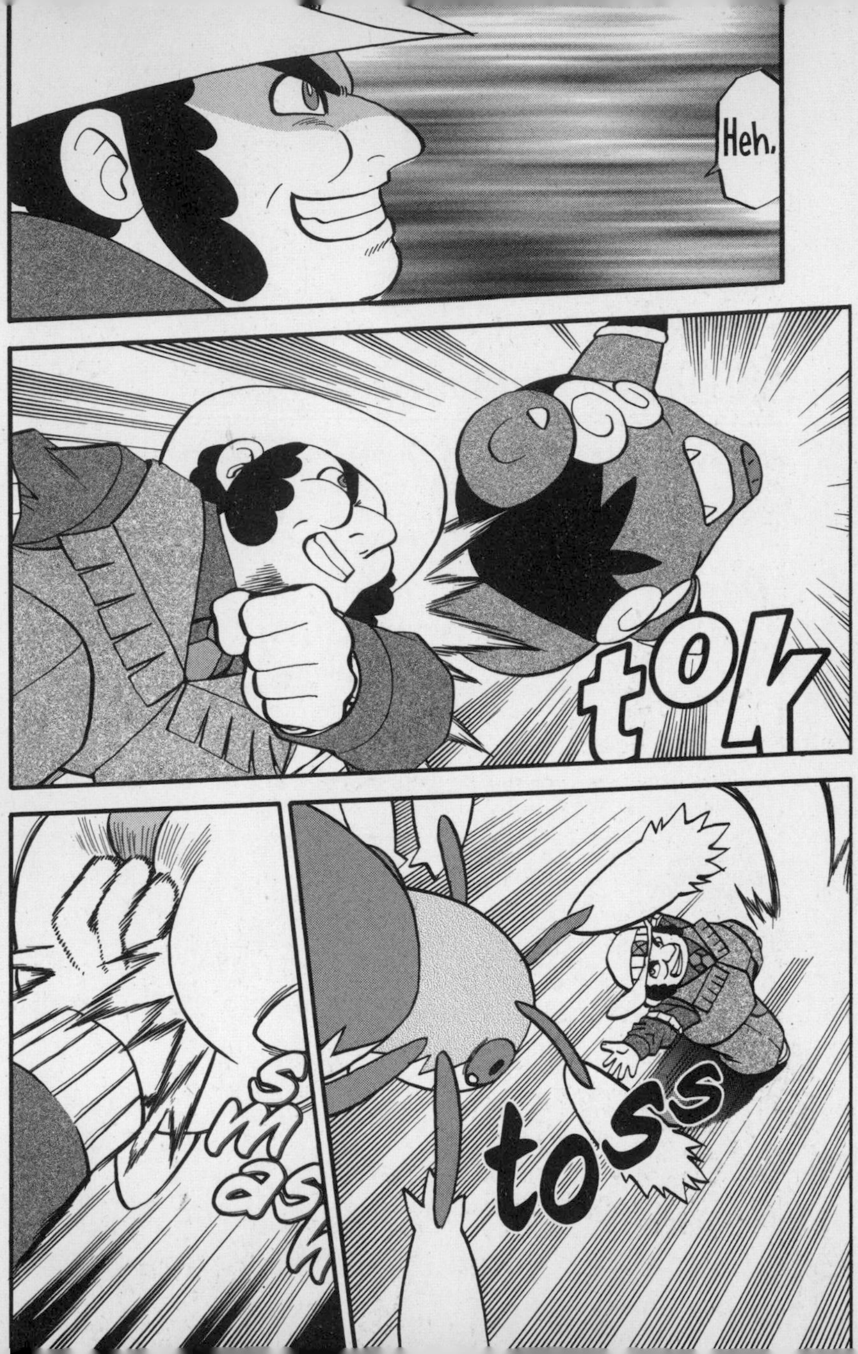
Heh.
tok
smash
toss

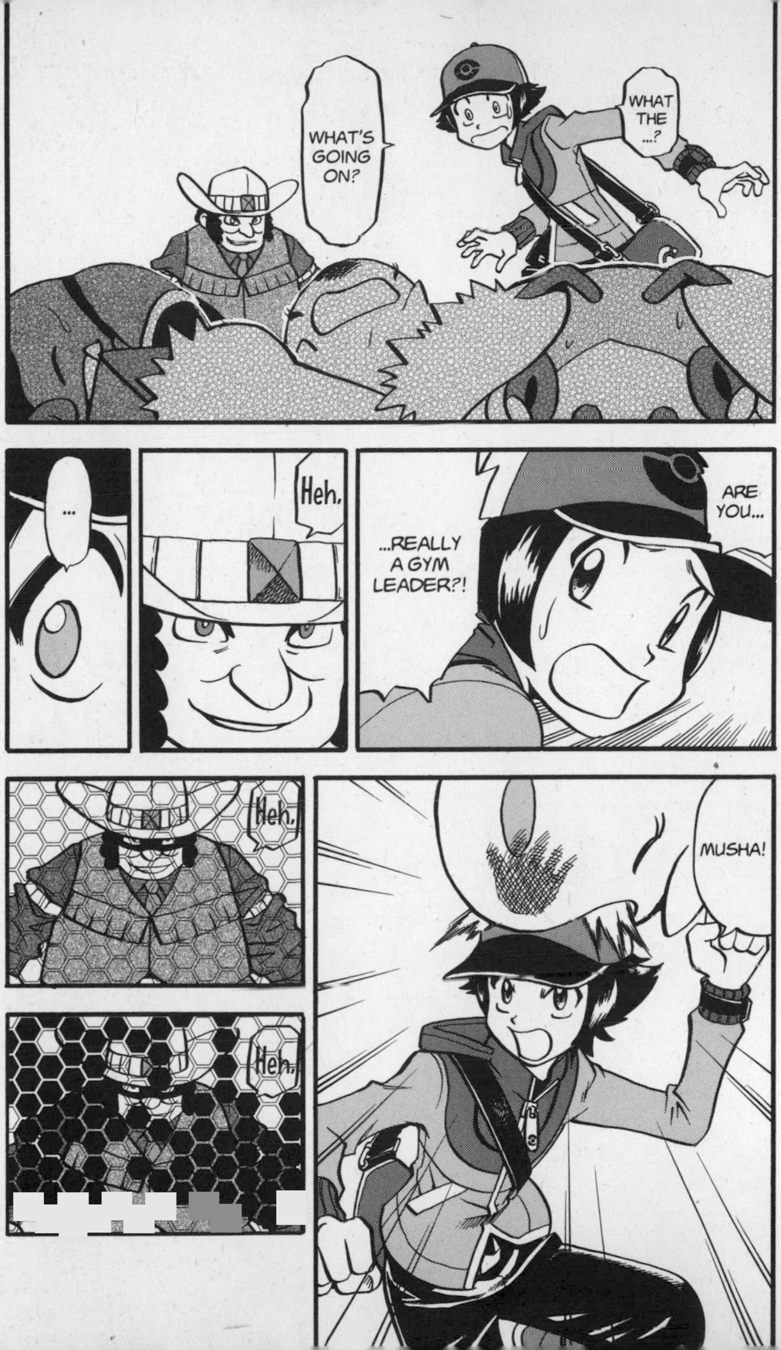
WHAT'S GOING ON?
WHAT THE ...?
...
Heh.
ARE YOU...
...REALLY A GYM LEADER?!
Heh.
Heh.
MUSHA!

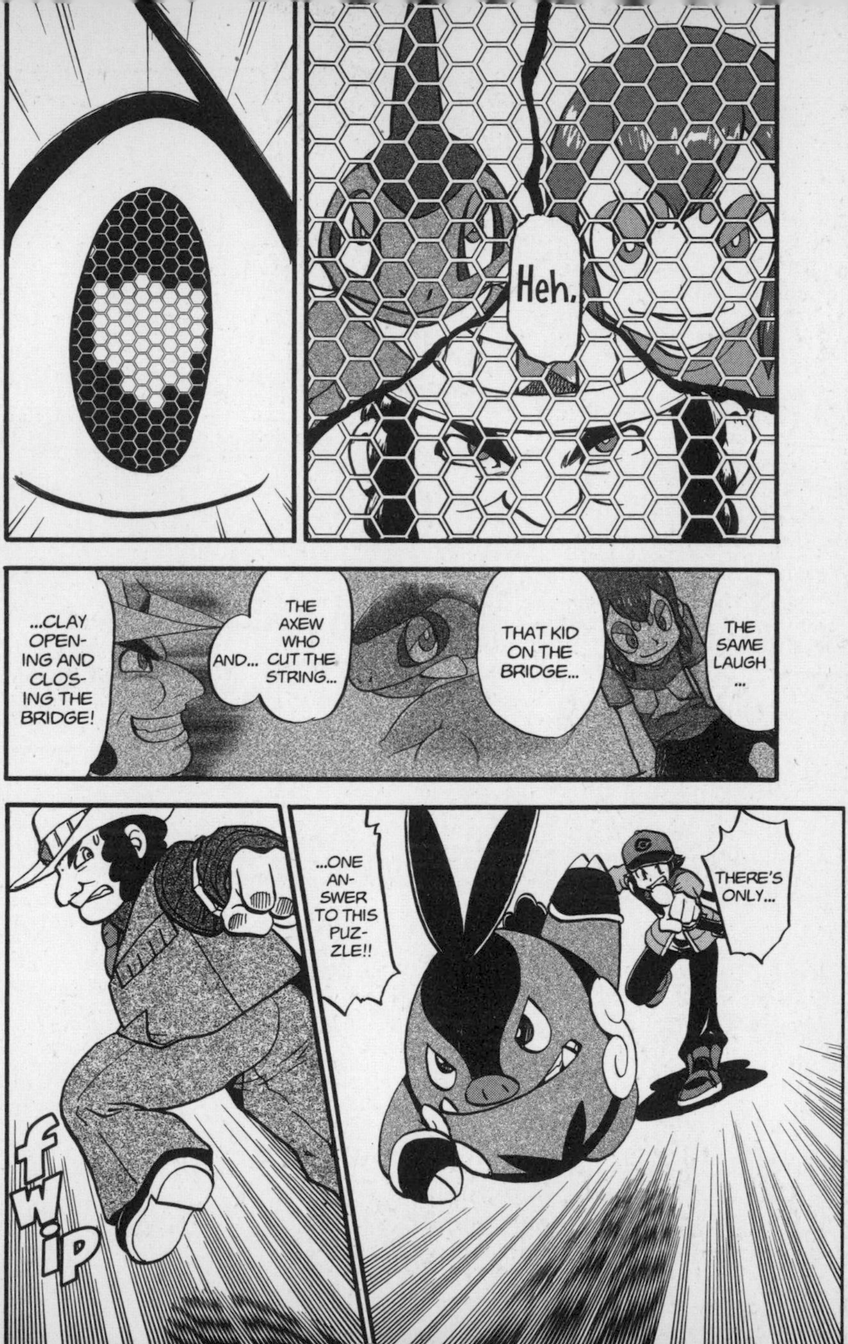
Heh.
THE SAME LAUGH ...
THAT KID ON THE BRIDGE...
AND... THE AXEW WHO CUT THE STRING...
...CLAY OPENING AND CLOSING THE BRIDGE!
THERE'S ONLY...
...ONE ANSWER TO THIS PUZZLE!!
fwip

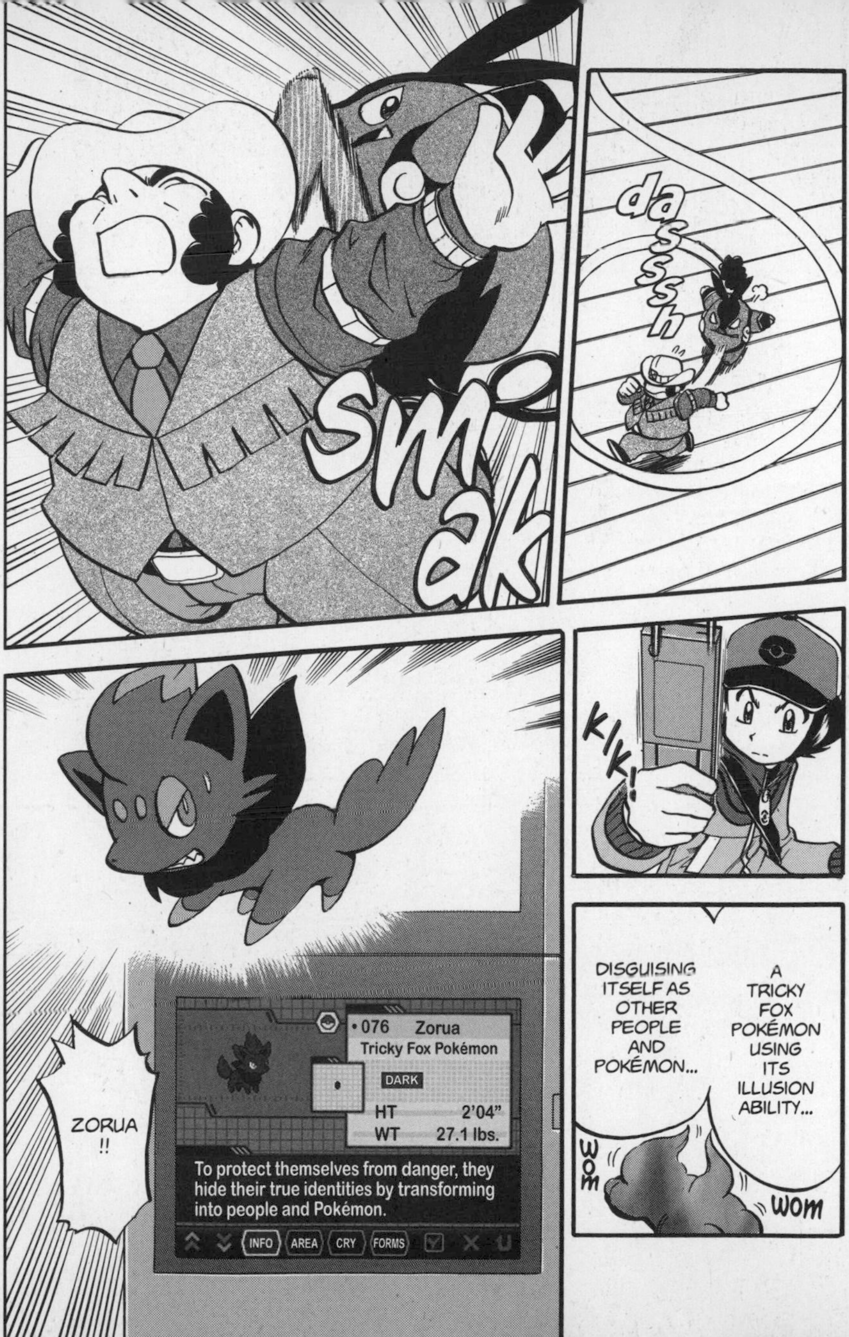
dasssh
smak
kik!
ZORUA !!
•076 Zorua
Tricky Fox Pokémon
DARK
HT 2'04"
WT 27.1 lbs.
To protect themselves from danger, they hide their true identities by transforming into people and Pokémon.
INFO AREA CRY FORMS
A TRICKY FOX POKÉMON USING ITS ILLUSION ABILITY...
DISGUISING ITSELF AS OTHER PEOPLE AND POKÉMON...
wom
wom

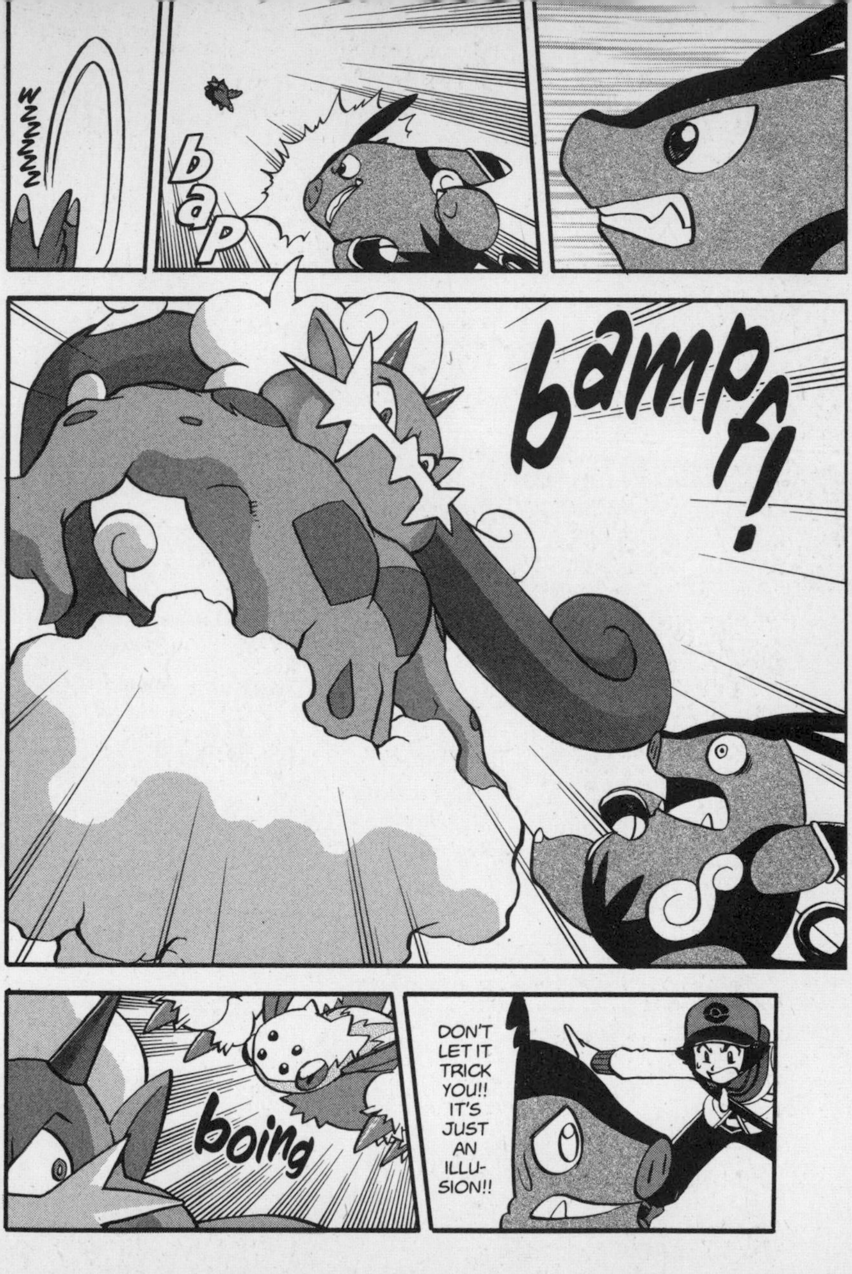
WZZZZZ
bap
bampf!
boing
DON'T LET IT TRICK YOU!! IT'S JUST AN ILLUSION!!

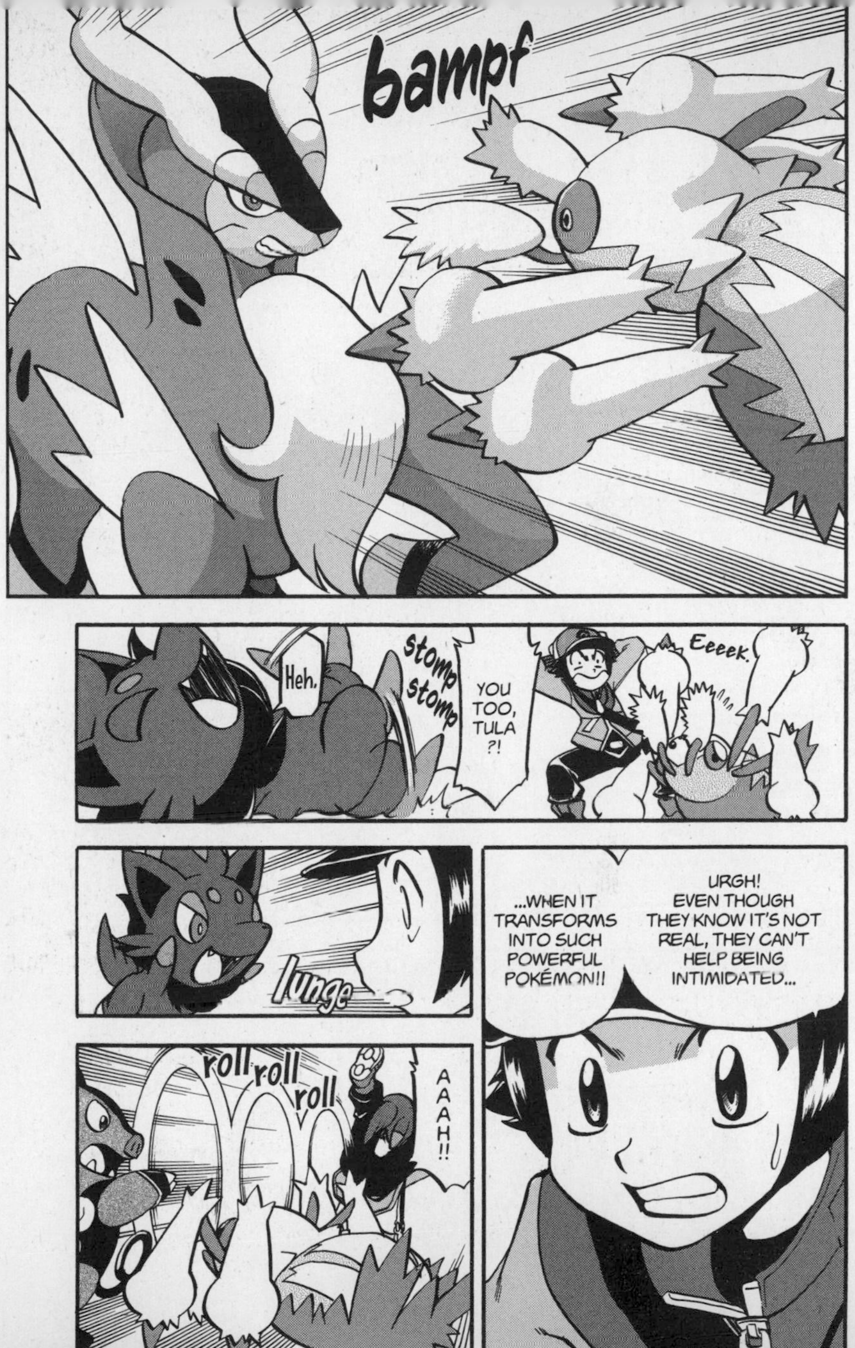
bampf
Heh.
stomp stomp
YOU TOO, TULA?!
Eeeek.
lunge
...WHEN IT TRANSFORMS INTO SUCH POWERFUL POKÉMON!!
URGH! EVEN THOUGH THEY KNOW IT'S NOT REAL, THEY CAN'T HELP BEING INTIMIDATED...
roll roll roll
AAAAH!!

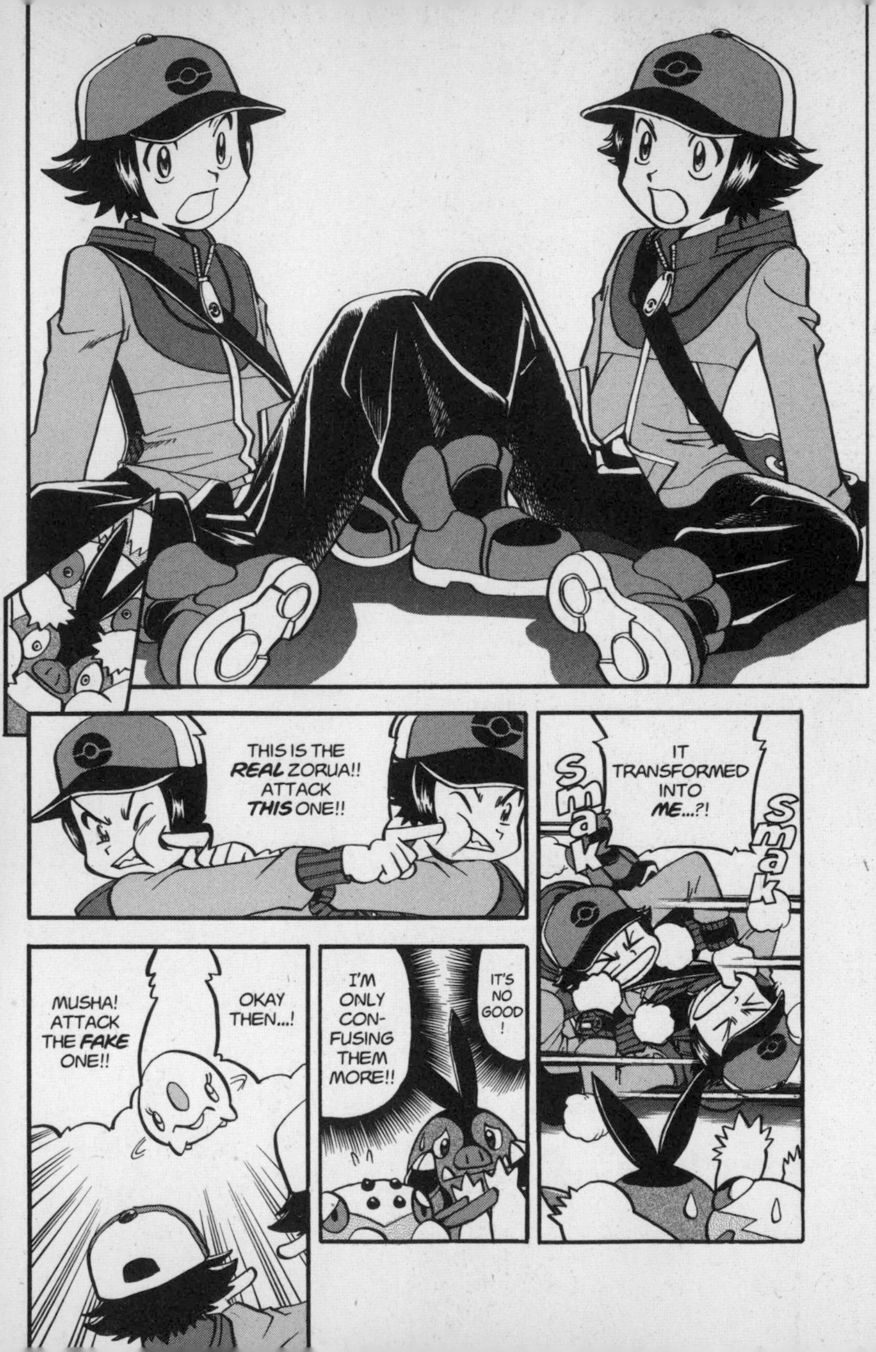
IT TRANSFORMED INTO ME...?!
SMAK
SMAK
THIS IS THE REAL ZORUA!! ATTACK THIS ONE!!
IT'S NO GOOD!
I'M ONLY CONFUSING THEM MORE!!
OKAY THEN...!
MUSHA! ATTACK THE FAKE ONE!!

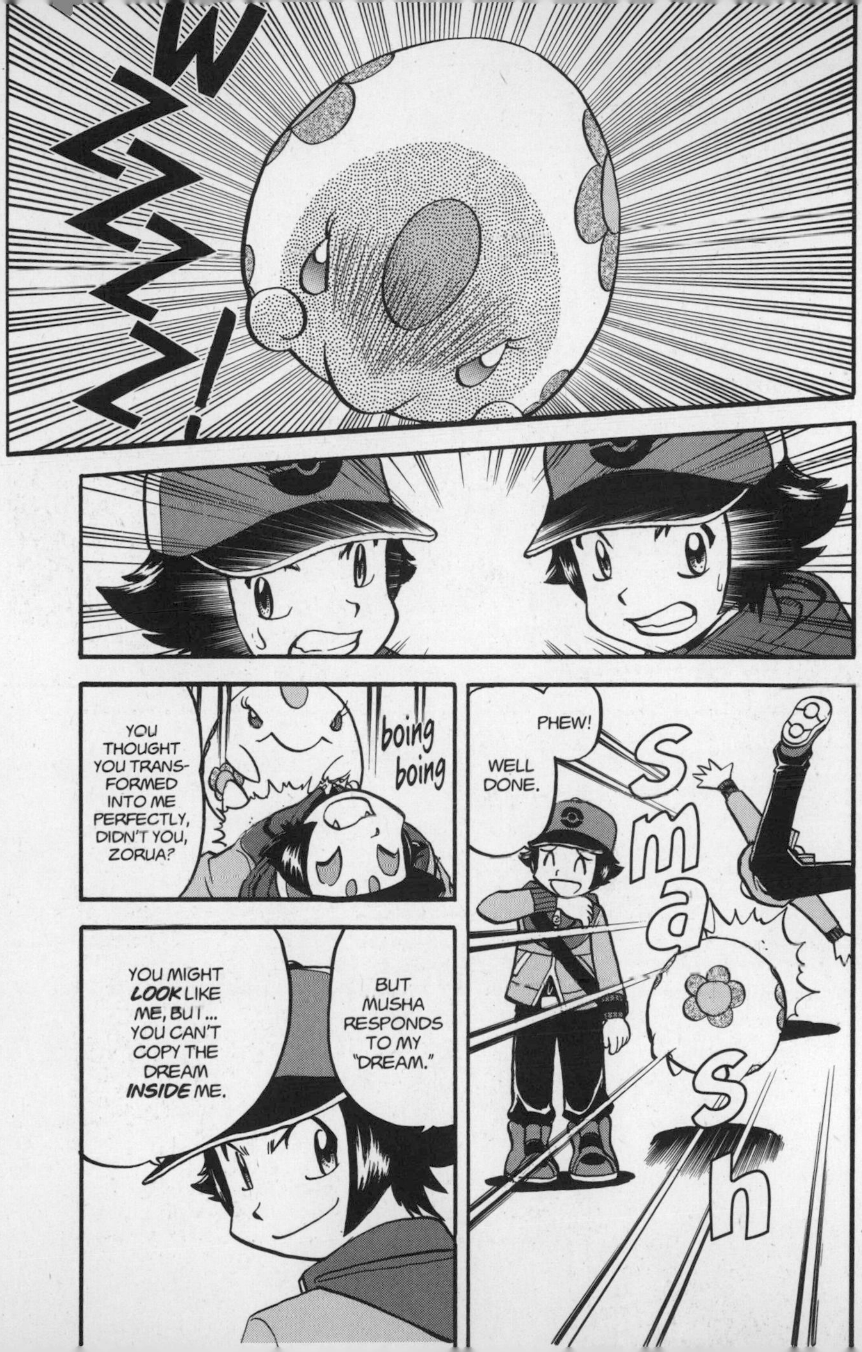
WMMMM!
YOU THOUGHT YOU TRANS-FORMED INTO ME PERFECTLY, DIDN'T YOU, ZORUA?
boing boing
PHEW!
WELL DONE.
Smash
YOU MIGHT LOOK LIKE ME, BUT... YOU CAN'T COPY THE DREAM INSIDE ME.
BUT MUSHA RESPONDS TO MY "DREAM."

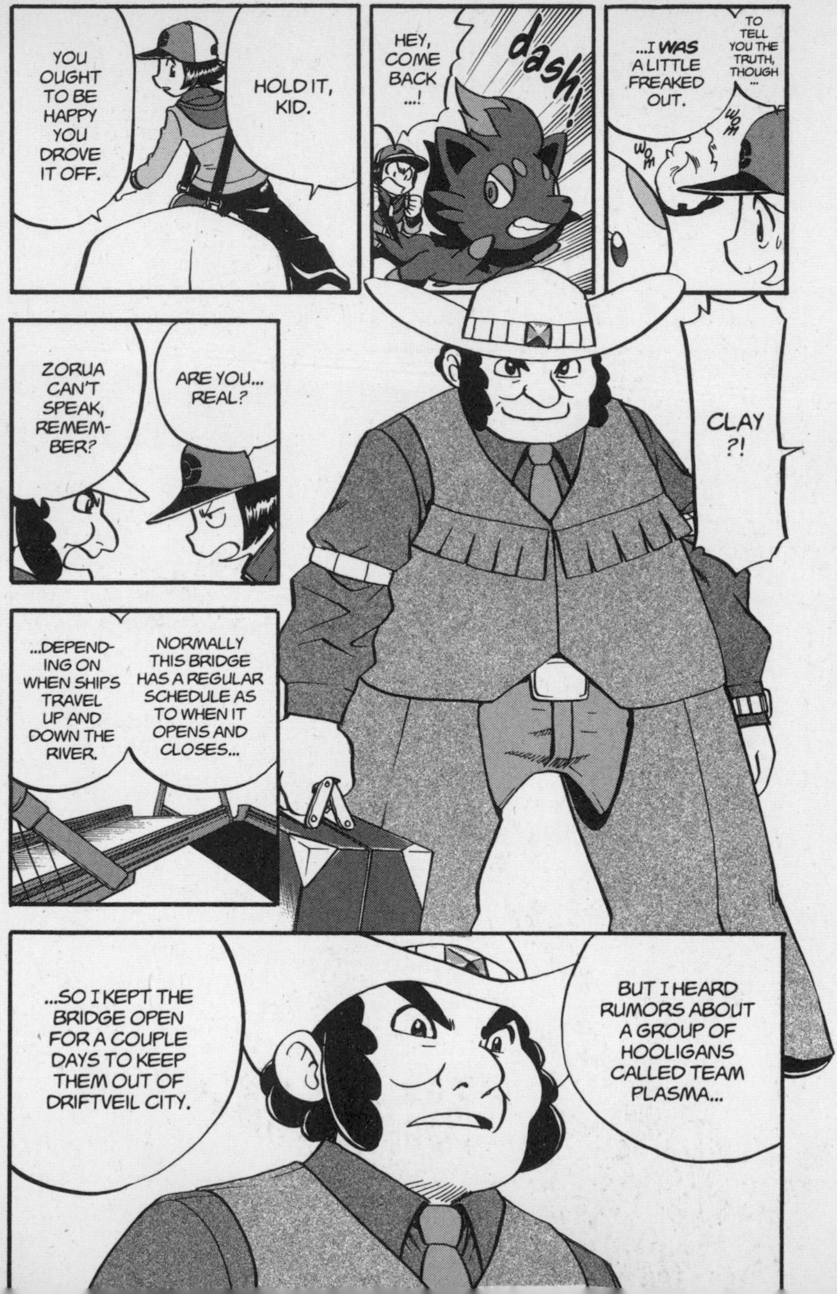
HOLD IT, KID.
YOU OUGHT TO BE HAPPY YOU DROVE IT OFF.
HEY, COME BACK ...!
dash!
TO TELL YOU THE TRUTH, THOUGH ...
...I WAS A LITTLE FREAKED OUT.
ARE YOU... REAL?
ZORUA CAN'T SPEAK, REMEMBER?
CLAY ?!
NORMALLY THIS BRIDGE HAS A REGULAR SCHEDULE AS TO WHEN IT OPENS AND CLOSES...
...DEPENDING ON WHEN SHIPS TRAVEL UP AND DOWN THE RIVER.
BUT I HEARD RUMORS ABOUT A GROUP OF HOOLIGANS CALLED TEAM PLASMA...
...SO I KEPT THE BRIDGE OPEN FOR A COUPLE DAYS TO KEEP THEM OUT OF DRIFTVEIL CITY.

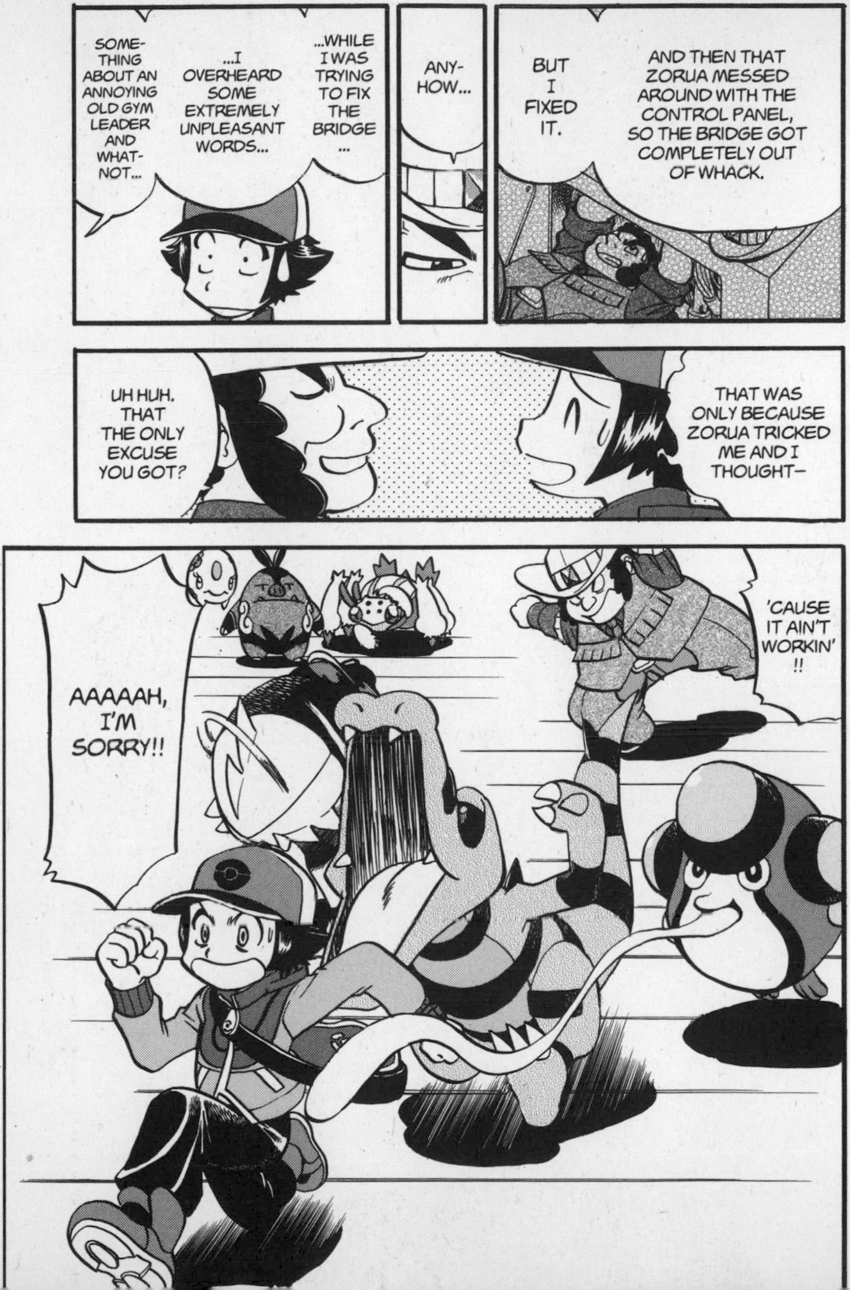
SOME-THING ABOUT AN ANNOYING OLD GYM LEADER AND WHAT-NOT...
...I OVERHEARD SOME EXTREMELY UNPLEASANT WORDS...
...WHILE I WAS TRYING TO FIX THE BRIDGE...
ANY-HOW...
BUT I FIXED IT.
AND THEN THAT ZORUA MESSED AROUND WITH THE CONTROL PANEL, SO THE BRIDGE GOT COMPLETELY OUT OF WHACK.
UH HUH. THAT THE ONLY EXCUSE YOU GOT?
THAT WAS ONLY BECAUSE ZORUA TRICKED ME AND I THOUGHT—
AAAAAH, I'M SORRY!!
'CAUSE IT AIN'T WORKIN'!!

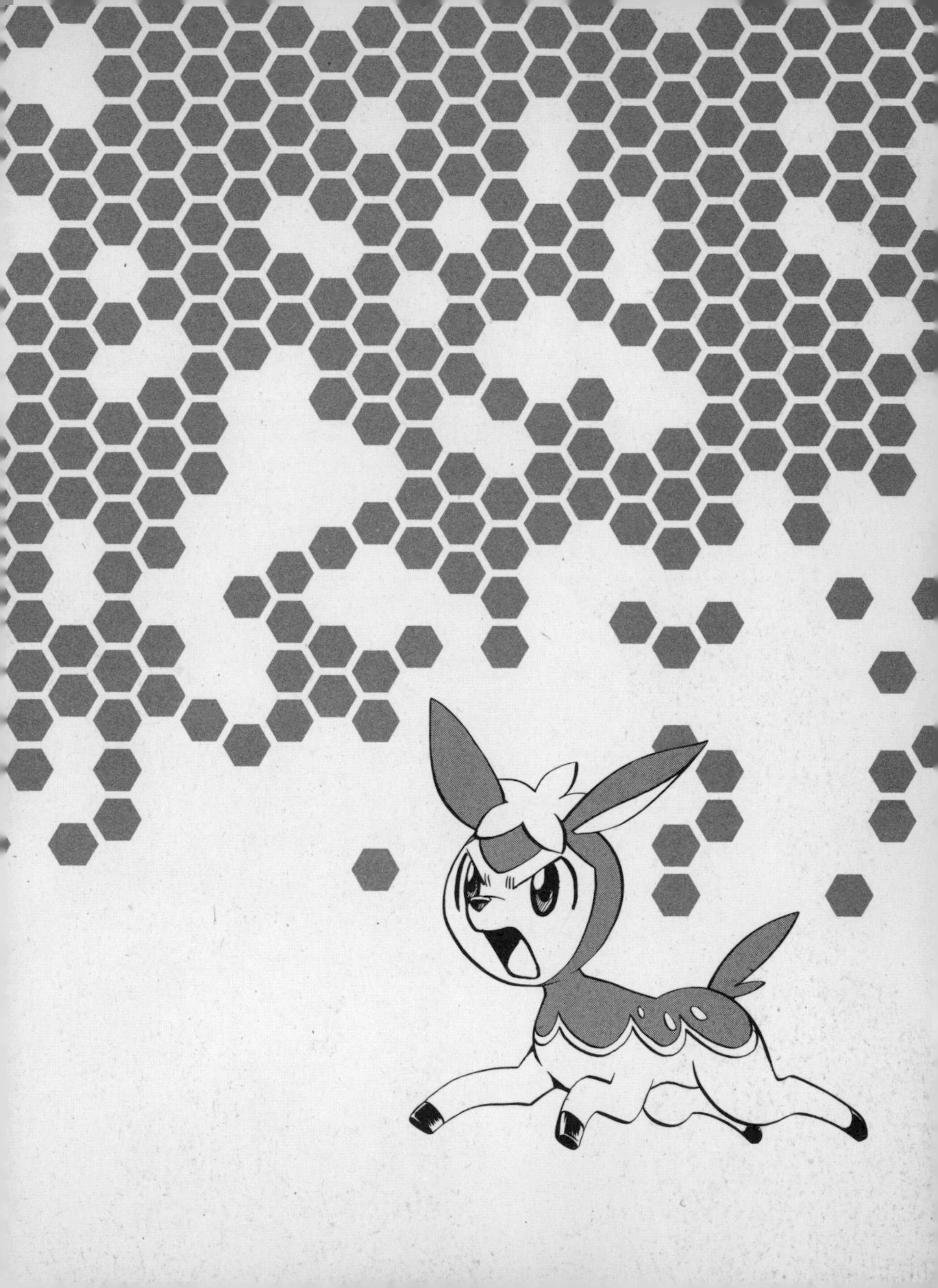

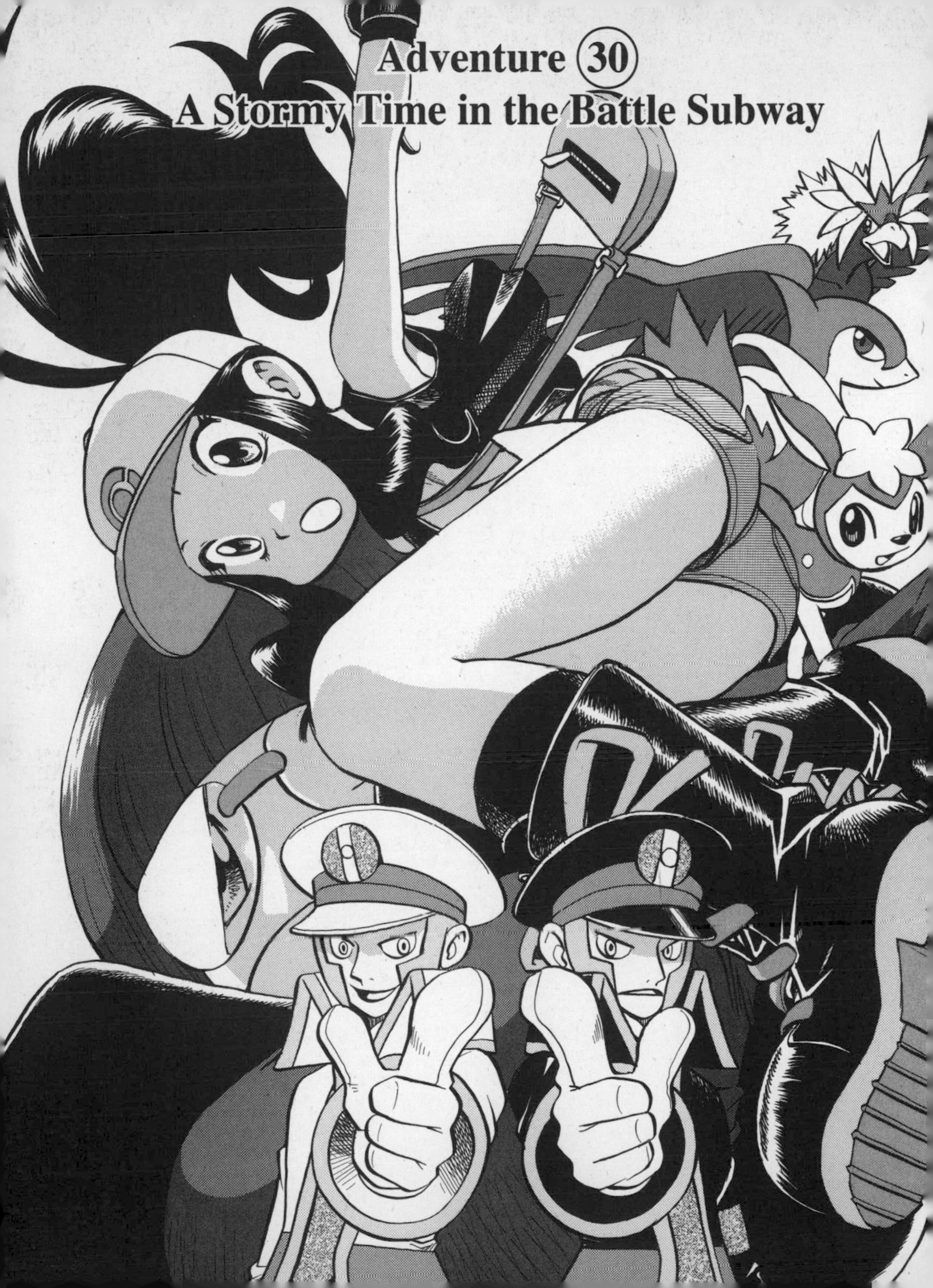
Adventure 30
A Stormy Time in the Battle Subway

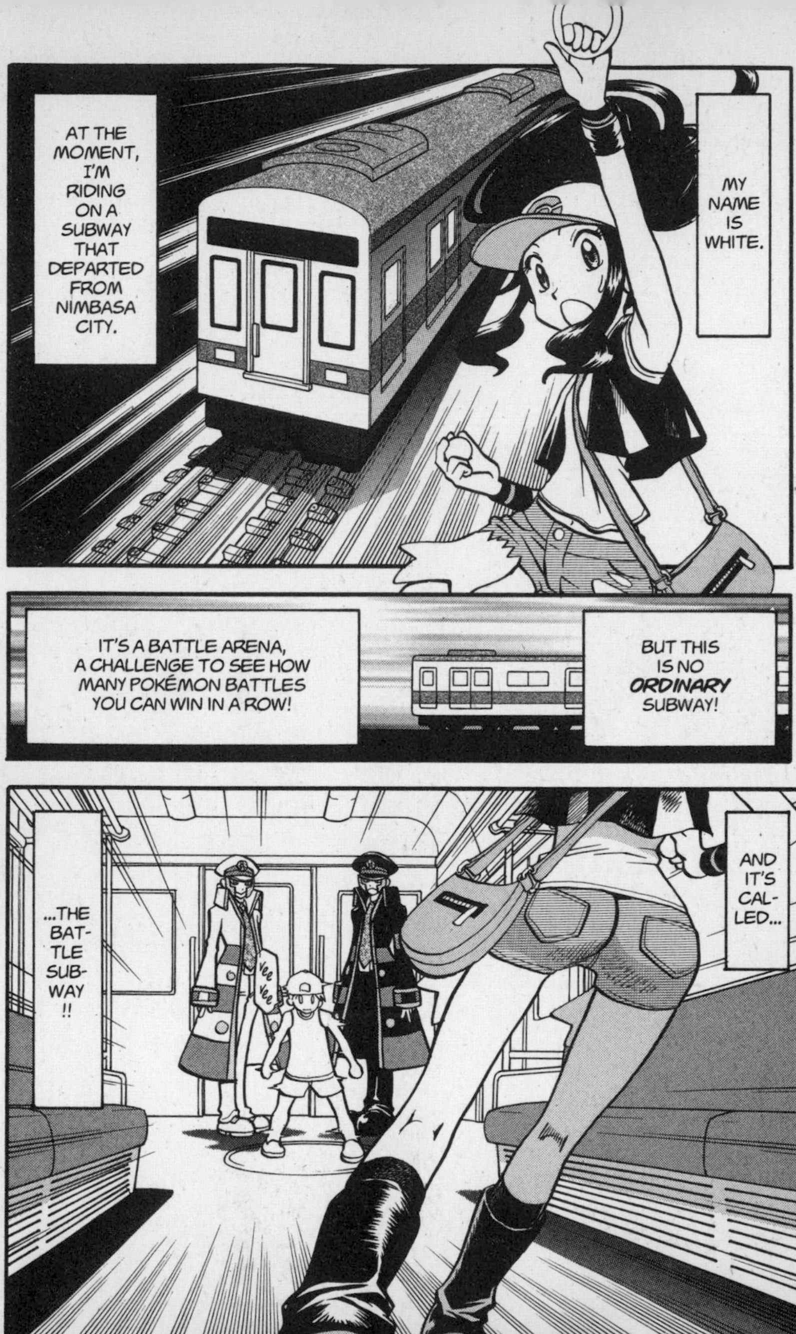
MY NAME IS WHITE.
AT THE MOMENT, I'M RIDING ON A SUBWAY THAT DEPARTED FROM NIMBASA CITY.
BUT THIS IS NO *ORDINARY* SUBWAY!
IT'S A BATTLE ARENA, A CHALLENGE TO SEE HOW MANY POKÉMON BATTLES YOU CAN WIN IN A ROW!
AND IT'S CAL-LED...
vee vee
...THE BAT-TLE SUB-WAY!!

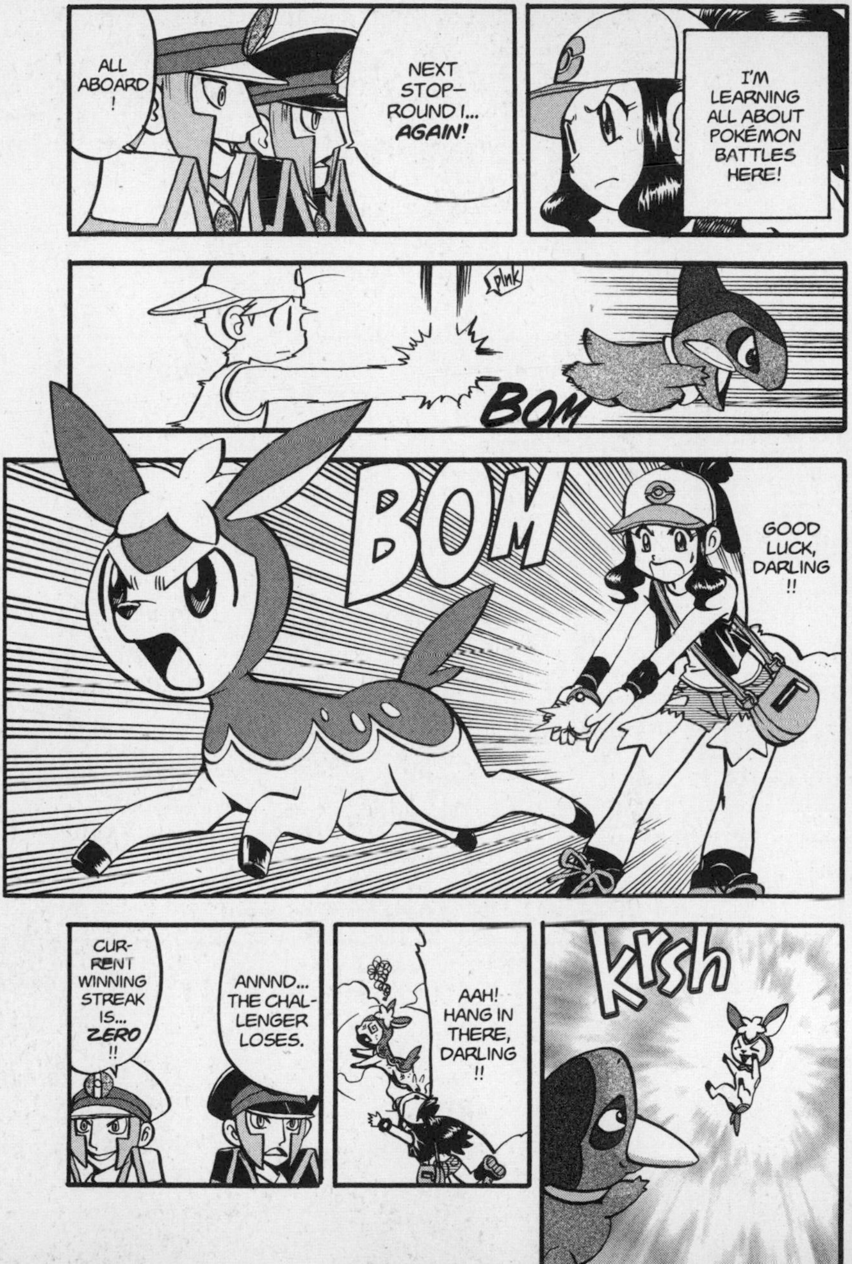
ALL ABOARD !
NEXT STOP—ROUND 1... AGAIN!
I'M LEARNING ALL ABOUT POKÉMON BATTLES HERE!
plink
BOM
BOM
GOOD LUCK, DARLING !!
CUR-RENT WINNING STREAK IS... ZERO !!
ANNND... THE CHAL-LENGER LOSES.
AAH! HANG IN THERE, DARLING !!
krsh

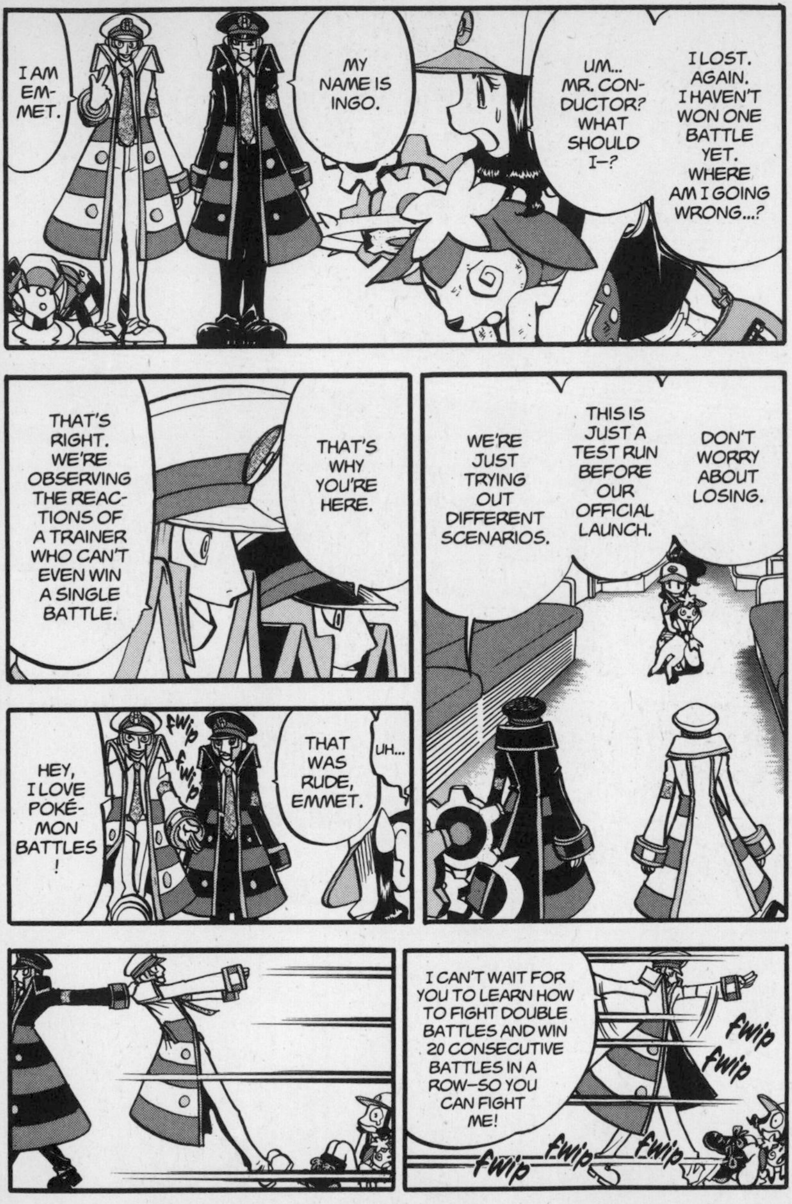
I AM EMMET.
MY NAME IS INGO.
UM... MR. CONDUCTOR? WHAT SHOULD I–?
I LOST. AGAIN. I HAVEN'T WON ONE BATTLE YET. WHERE AM I GOING WRONG...?
THAT'S RIGHT. WE'RE OBSERVING THE REACTIONS OF A TRAINER WHO CAN'T EVEN WIN A SINGLE BATTLE.
THAT'S WHY YOU'RE HERE.
WE'RE JUST TRYING OUT DIFFERENT SCENARIOS.
THIS IS JUST A TEST RUN BEFORE OUR OFFICIAL LAUNCH.
DON'T WORRY ABOUT LOSING.
HEY, I LOVE POKÉMON BATTLES!
fwip fwip
THAT WAS RUDE, EMMET.
UH...
I CAN'T WAIT FOR YOU TO LEARN HOW TO FIGHT DOUBLE BATTLES AND WIN 20 CONSECUTIVE BATTLES IN A ROW–SO YOU CAN FIGHT ME!
fwip fwip
fwip fwip fwip

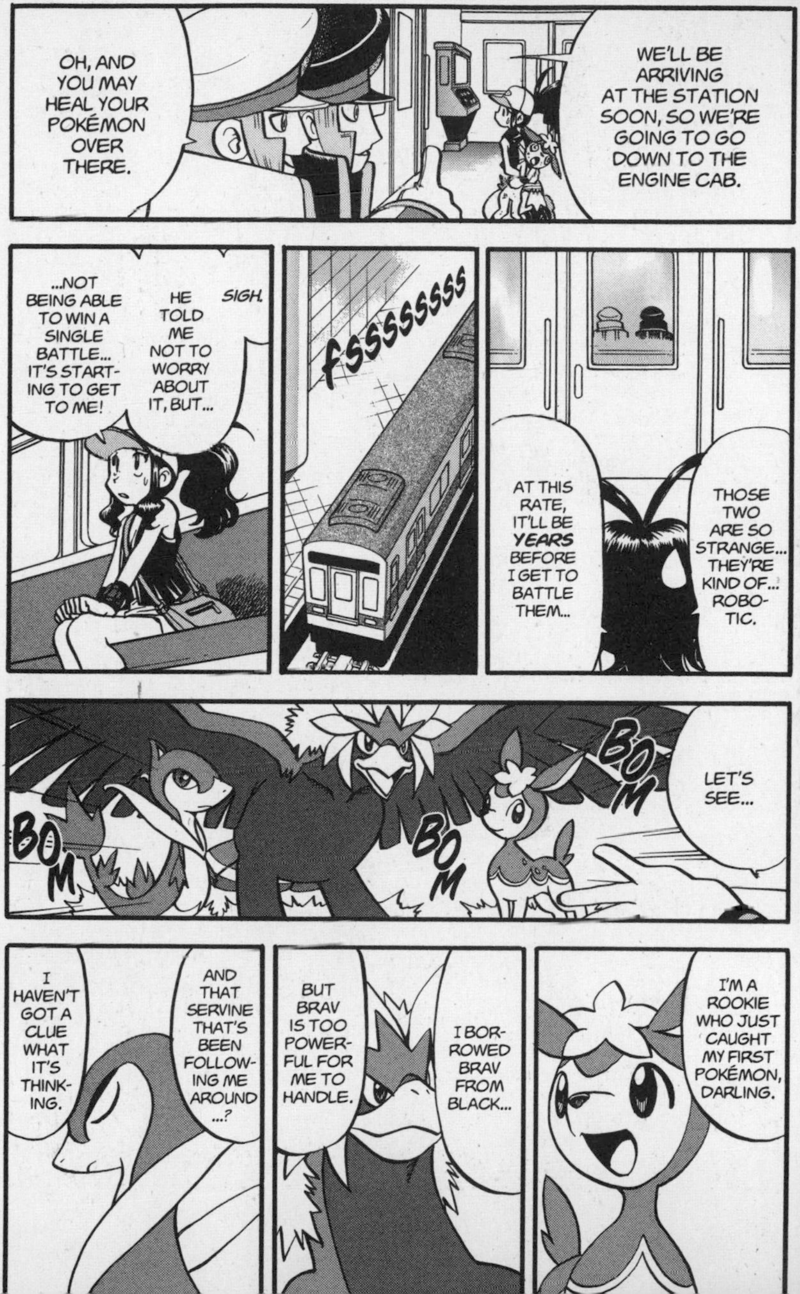
WE'LL BE ARRIVING AT THE STATION SOON, SO WE'RE GOING TO GO DOWN TO THE ENGINE CAB.
OH, AND YOU MAY HEAL YOUR POKÉMON OVER THERE.
THOSE TWO ARE SO STRANGE... THEY'RE KIND OF... ROBO-TIC.
AT THIS RATE, IT'LL BE *YEARS* BEFORE I GET TO BATTLE THEM...
fSSSSSSSS
SIGH.
HE TOLD ME NOT TO WORRY ABOUT IT, BUT...
...NOT BEING ABLE TO WIN A SINGLE BATTLE... IT'S START-ING TO GET TO ME!
LET'S SEE...
BOM
BOM
BOM
I'M A ROOKIE WHO JUST CAUGHT MY FIRST POKÉMON, DARLING.
I BOR-ROWED BRAV FROM BLACK...
BUT BRAV IS TOO POWER-FUL FOR ME TO HANDLE.
AND THAT SERVINE THAT'S BEEN FOLLOW-ING ME AROUND ...?
I HAVEN'T GOT A CLUE WHAT IT'S THINK-ING.

WOO WOO

TRAIN DE-PART-ING!

MY OPPONENTS ARE ALL COMPUTER GENERATED, SO... I OUGHT TO JUST TAKE MY TIME AND LEARN FROM MY MISTAKES.

IT'S OKAY, THOUGH. I'M A BEGINNER. THERE'S NOTHING WRONG WITH ME NOT WINNING BATTLES.

Zhuum zhumm

OH!

WHAT A NICE CHANGE OF ATMO-SPHERE.

I GUESS THIS SUBWAY DOESN'T STAY UNDER-GROUND ALL THE TIME!

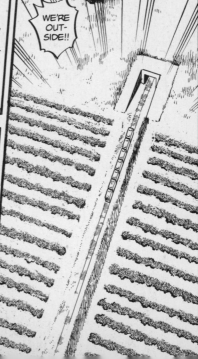

WE'RE OUT-SIDE!!

"THE POKÉMON SOUNDED A SOFT CRY OF REASSUR-ANCE..."

"...LOOKED UP AT ITS TRAINER AND SAW THE SEEDS OF DOUBT TAKING ROOT AS TOGETHER THEY FACED THEIR TOUGHEST OPPONENT YET."

"THE TINY BUT STRONG POKÉ-MON..."

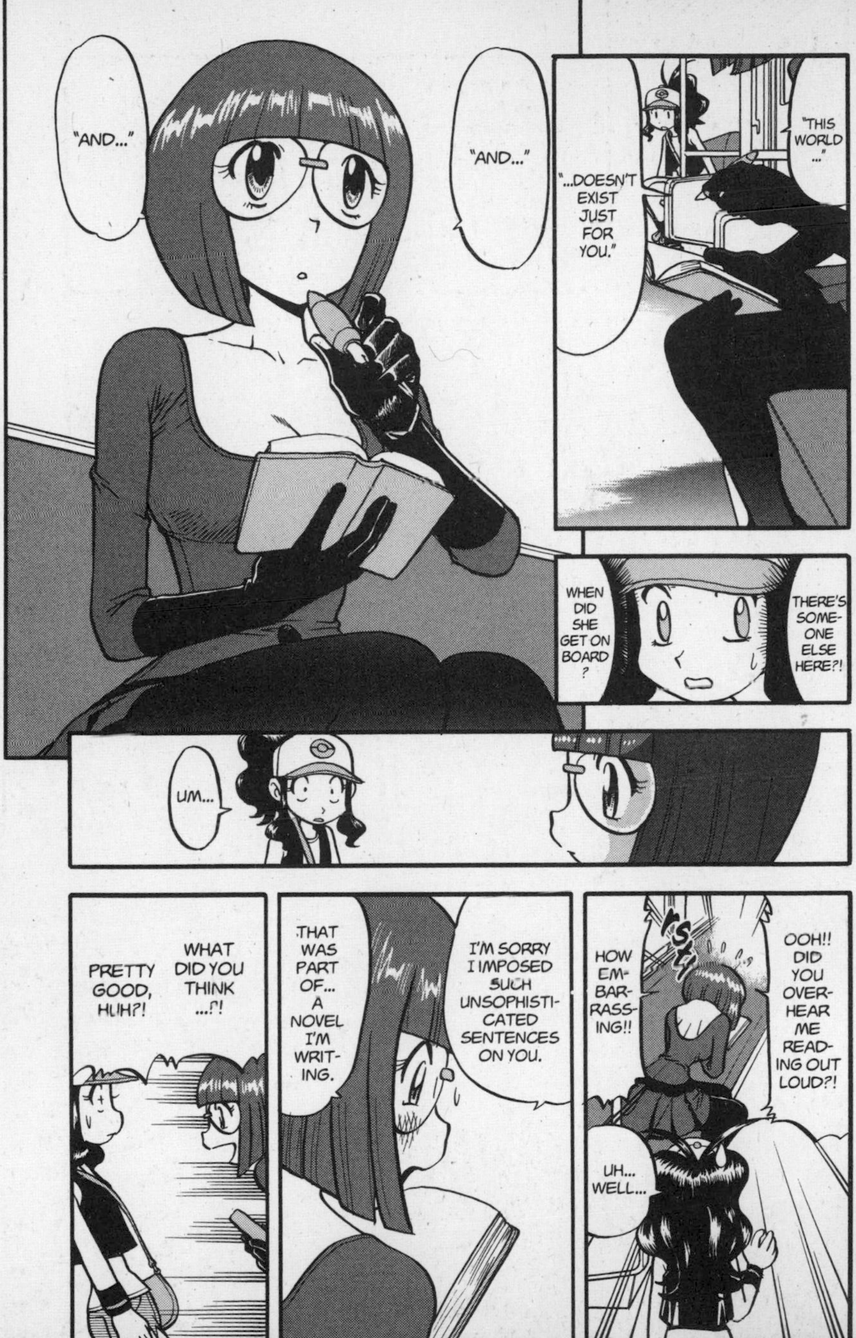
"THIS WORLD..."
"...DOESN'T EXIST JUST FOR YOU."
"AND..."
"AND..."
THERE'S SOME-ONE ELSE HERE?!
WHEN DID SHE GET ON BOARD?
UM...
OOH!! DID YOU OVER-HEAR ME READ-ING OUT LOUD?!
HOW EM-BAR-RASS-ING!!
UH... WELL...
I'M SORRY I IMPOSED SUCH UNSOPHISTI-CATED SENTENCES ON YOU.
THAT WAS PART OF... A NOVEL I'M WRIT-ING.
WHAT DID YOU THINK ...?!
PRETTY GOOD, HUH?!

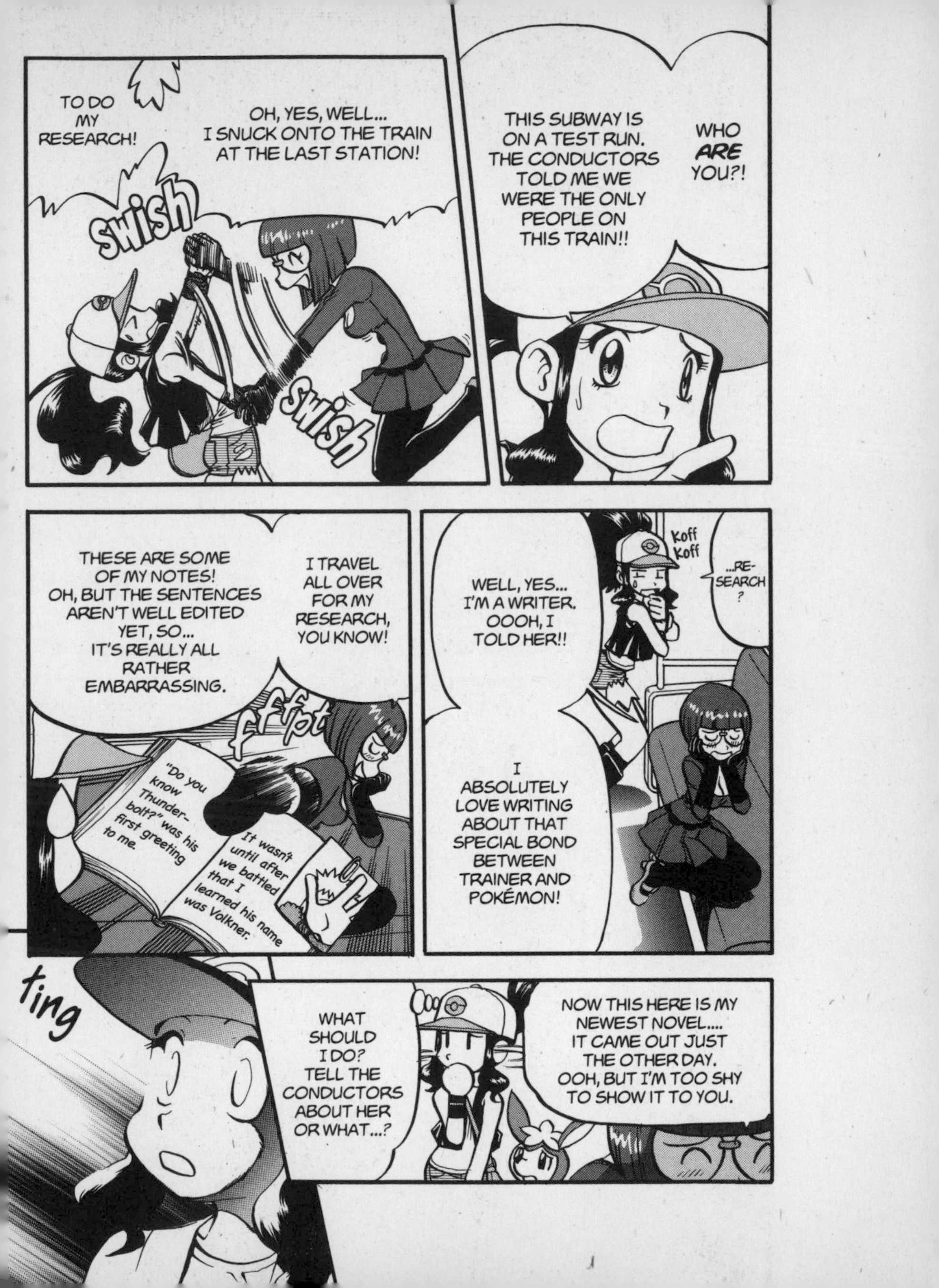

WHO ARE YOU?!
THIS SUBWAY IS ON A TEST RUN. THE CONDUCTORS TOLD ME WE WERE THE ONLY PEOPLE ON THIS TRAIN!!
OH, YES, WELL... I SNUCK ONTO THE TRAIN AT THE LAST STATION!
TO DO MY RESEARCH!
SWISH
SWISH
...RE-SEARCH?
KOFF KOFF
WELL, YES... I'M A WRITER. OOOH, I TOLD HER!!
I ABSOLUTELY LOVE WRITING ABOUT THAT SPECIAL BOND BETWEEN TRAINER AND POKÉMON!
I TRAVEL ALL OVER FOR MY RESEARCH, YOU KNOW!
THESE ARE SOME OF MY NOTES! OH, BUT THE SENTENCES AREN'T WELL EDITED YET, SO... IT'S REALLY ALL RATHER EMBARRASSING.
FFFPT
"Do you know Thunderbolt?" was his first greeting to me.
It wasn't until after we battled that I learned his name was Volkner.
NOW THIS HERE IS MY NEWEST NOVEL.... IT CAME OUT JUST THE OTHER DAY. OOH, BUT I'M TOO SHY TO SHOW IT TO YOU.
WHAT SHOULD I DO? TELL THE CONDUCTORS ABOUT HER OR WHAT...?
TING

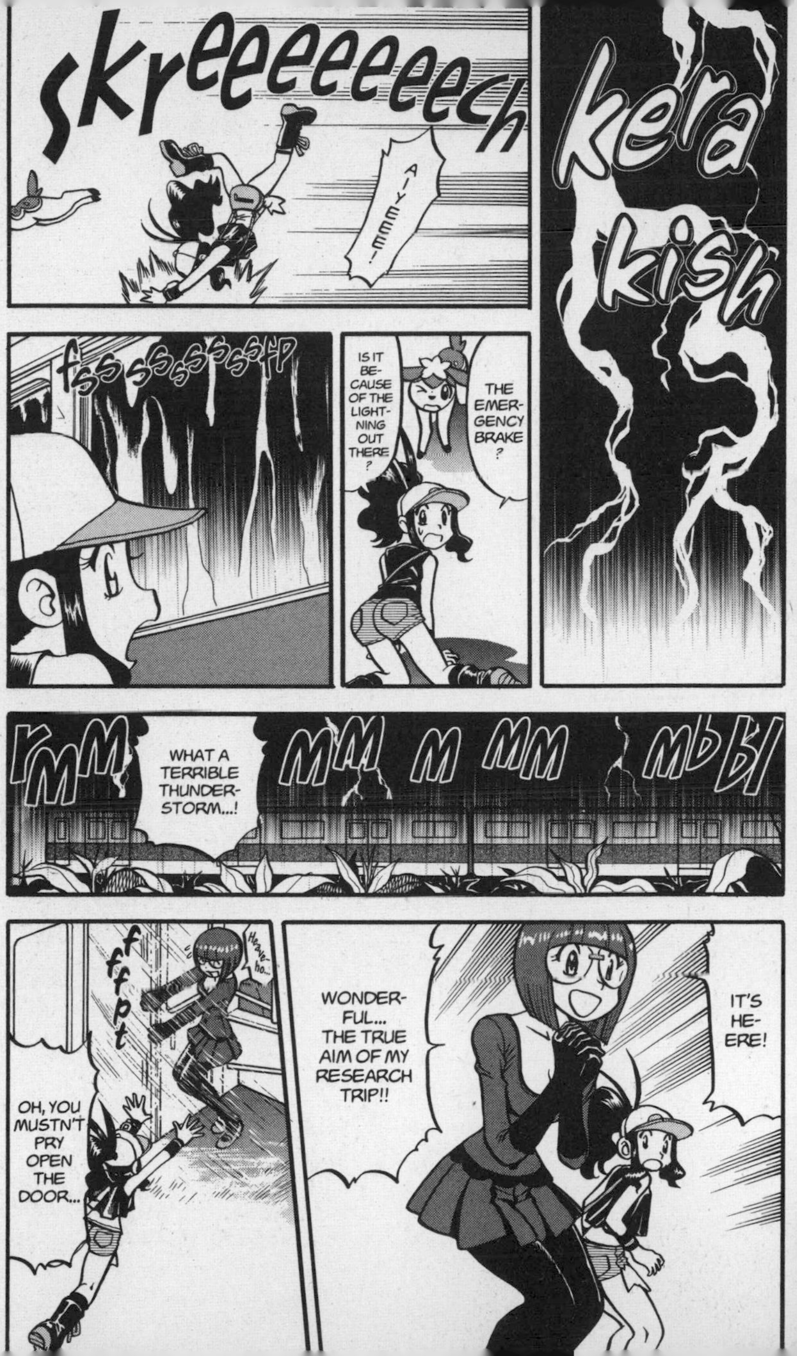
skreeeeeeeech
AIYEEE!
kera kish
fsssssssssfp
IS IT BE-CAUSE OF THE LIGHT-NING OUT THERE?
THE EMER-GENCY BRAKE?
rMM
WHAT A TERRIBLE THUNDER-STORM...!
MM M MM mbbl
ffffpt
Heave-ho...
OH, YOU MUSTN'T PRY OPEN THE DOOR...
WONDER-FUL... THE TRUE AIM OF MY RESEARCH TRIP!!
IT'S HE-ERE!

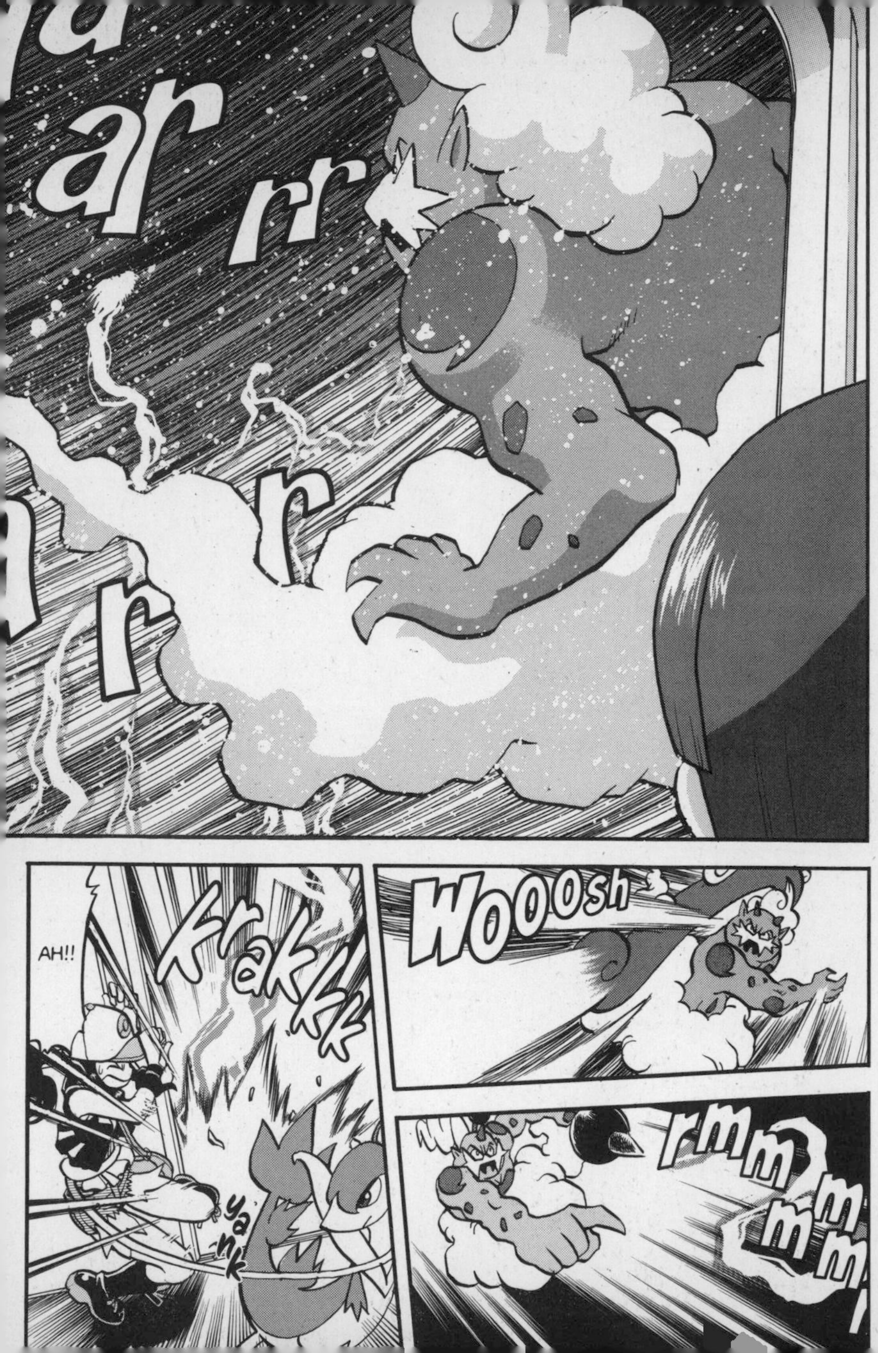

ar rr
r r
AH!!
krakkk
ya-nik
WOOOsh
rmmmmm

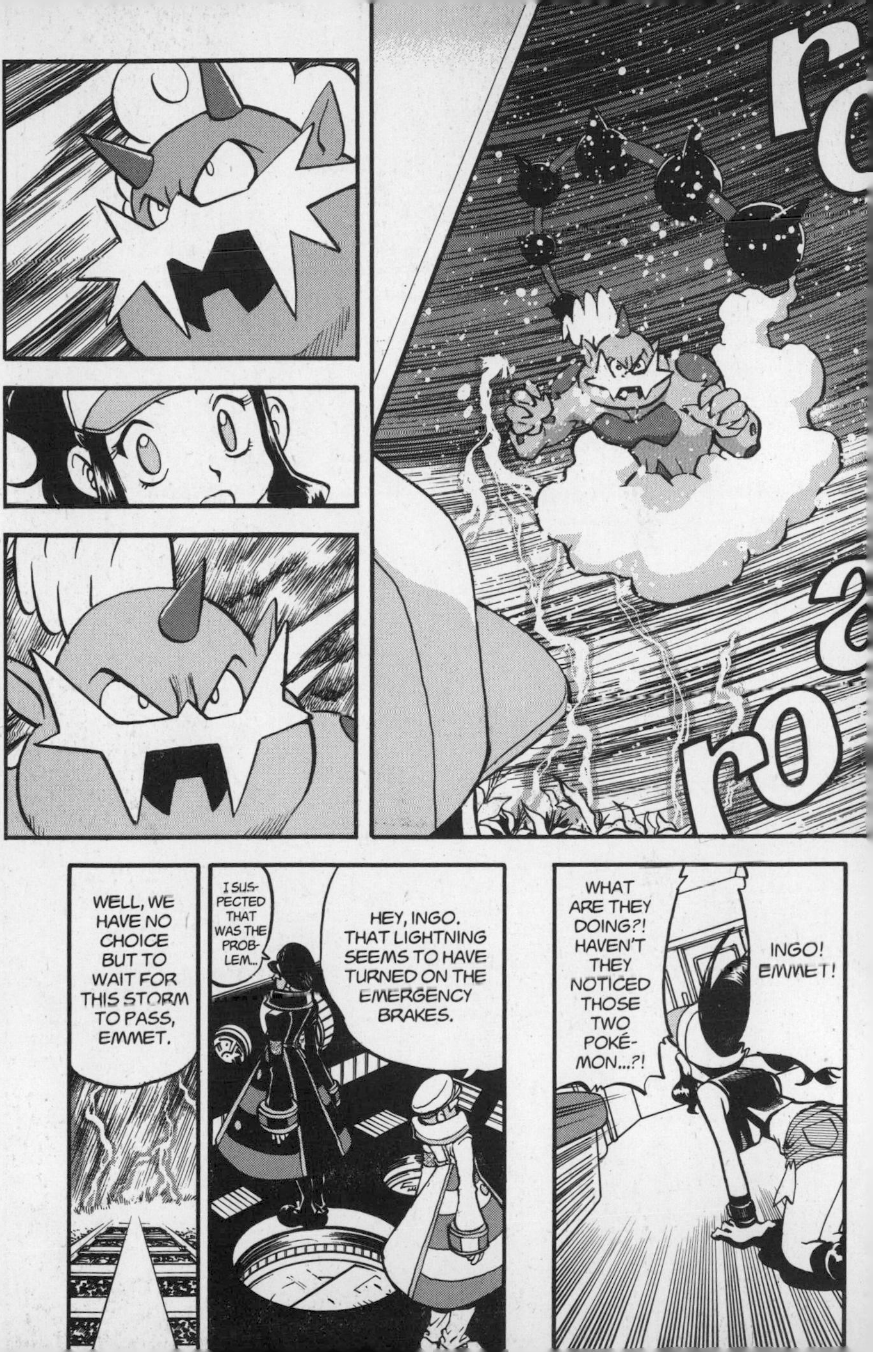
INGO! EMMET!
WHAT ARE THEY DOING?! HAVEN'T THEY NOTICED THOSE TWO POKÉMON...?!
HEY, INGO. THAT LIGHTNING SEEMS TO HAVE TURNED ON THE EMERGENCY BRAKES.
I SUSPECTED THAT WAS THE PROBLEM...
WELL, WE HAVE NO CHOICE BUT TO WAIT FOR THIS STORM TO PASS, EMMET.

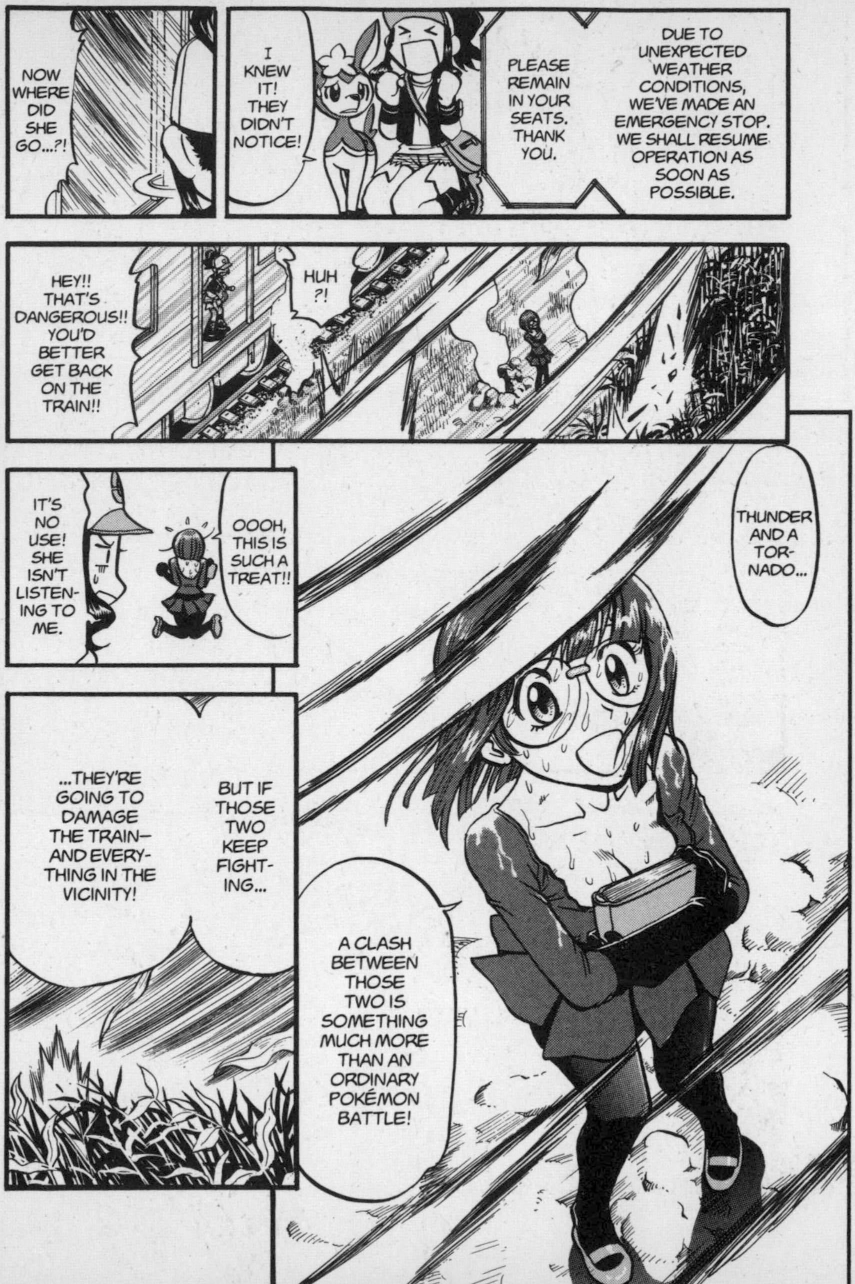
NOW WHERE DID SHE GO...?!
I KNEW IT! THEY DIDN'T NOTICE!
DUE TO UNEXPECTED WEATHER CONDITIONS, WE'VE MADE AN EMERGENCY STOP. WE SHALL RESUME OPERATION AS SOON AS POSSIBLE.
PLEASE REMAIN IN YOUR SEATS. THANK YOU.
HEY!! THAT'S DANGEROUS!! YOU'D BETTER GET BACK ON THE TRAIN!!
HUH ?!
IT'S NO USE! SHE ISN'T LISTENING TO ME.
OOOH, THIS IS SUCH A TREAT!!
THUNDER AND A TORNADO...
A CLASH BETWEEN THOSE TWO IS SOMETHING MUCH MORE THAN AN ORDINARY POKÉMON BATTLE!
BUT IF THOSE TWO KEEP FIGHTING...
...THEY'RE GOING TO DAMAGE THE TRAIN—AND EVERYTHING IN THE VICINITY!

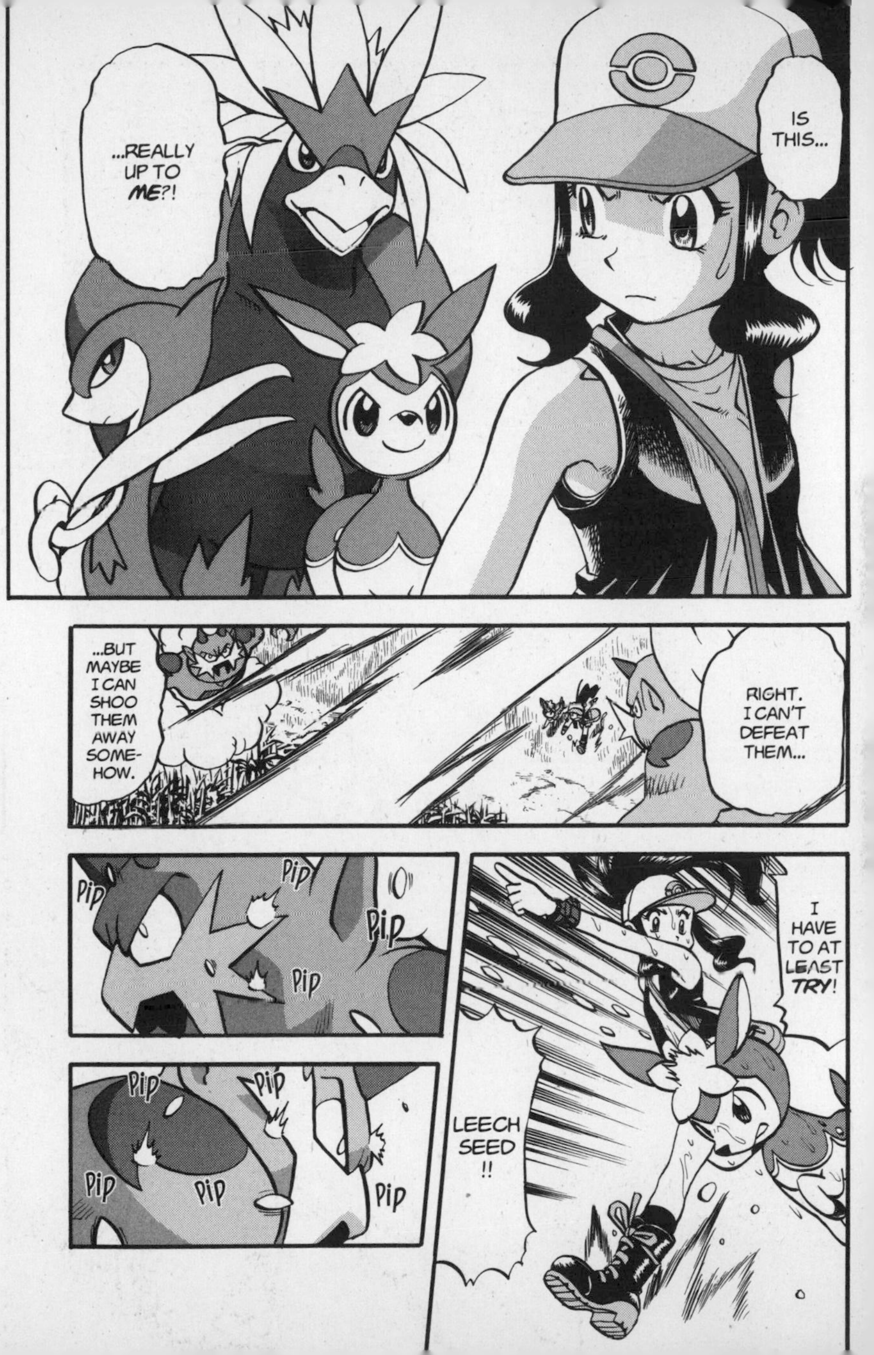
IS THIS...
...REALLY UP TO ME?!
RIGHT. I CAN'T DEFEAT THEM...
...BUT MAYBE I CAN SHOO THEM AWAY SOME-HOW.
I HAVE TO AT LEAST TRY!
LEECH SEED !!
Pip
Pip
Pip
Pip
Pip
Pip
Pip
Pip
Pip

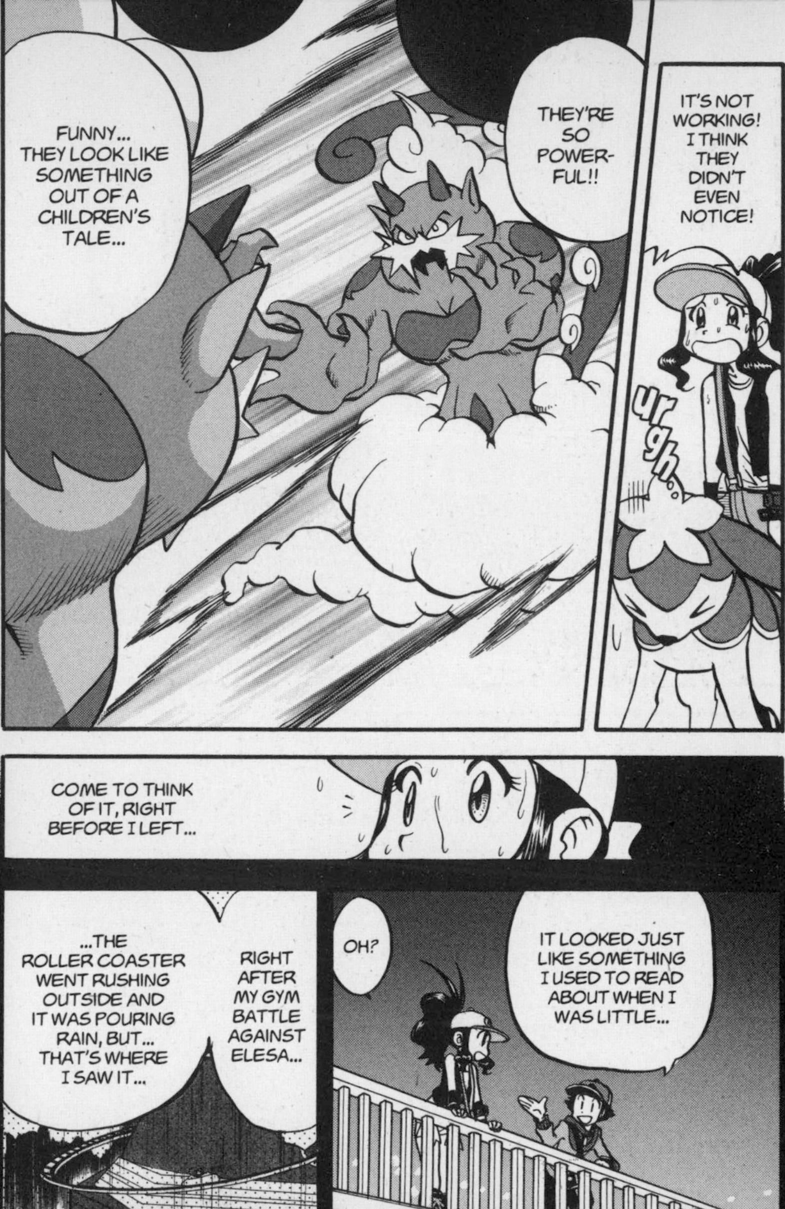
FUNNY... THEY LOOK LIKE SOMETHING OUT OF A CHILDREN'S TALE...
THEY'RE SO POWER-FUL!!
IT'S NOT WORKING! I THINK THEY DIDN'T EVEN NOTICE!
urgh...
COME TO THINK OF IT, RIGHT BEFORE I LEFT...
RIGHT AFTER MY GYM BATTLE AGAINST ELESA...
...THE ROLLER COASTER WENT RUSHING OUTSIDE AND IT WAS POURING RAIN, BUT... THAT'S WHERE I SAW IT...
IT LOOKED JUST LIKE SOMETHING I USED TO READ ABOUT WHEN I WAS LITTLE...
OH?

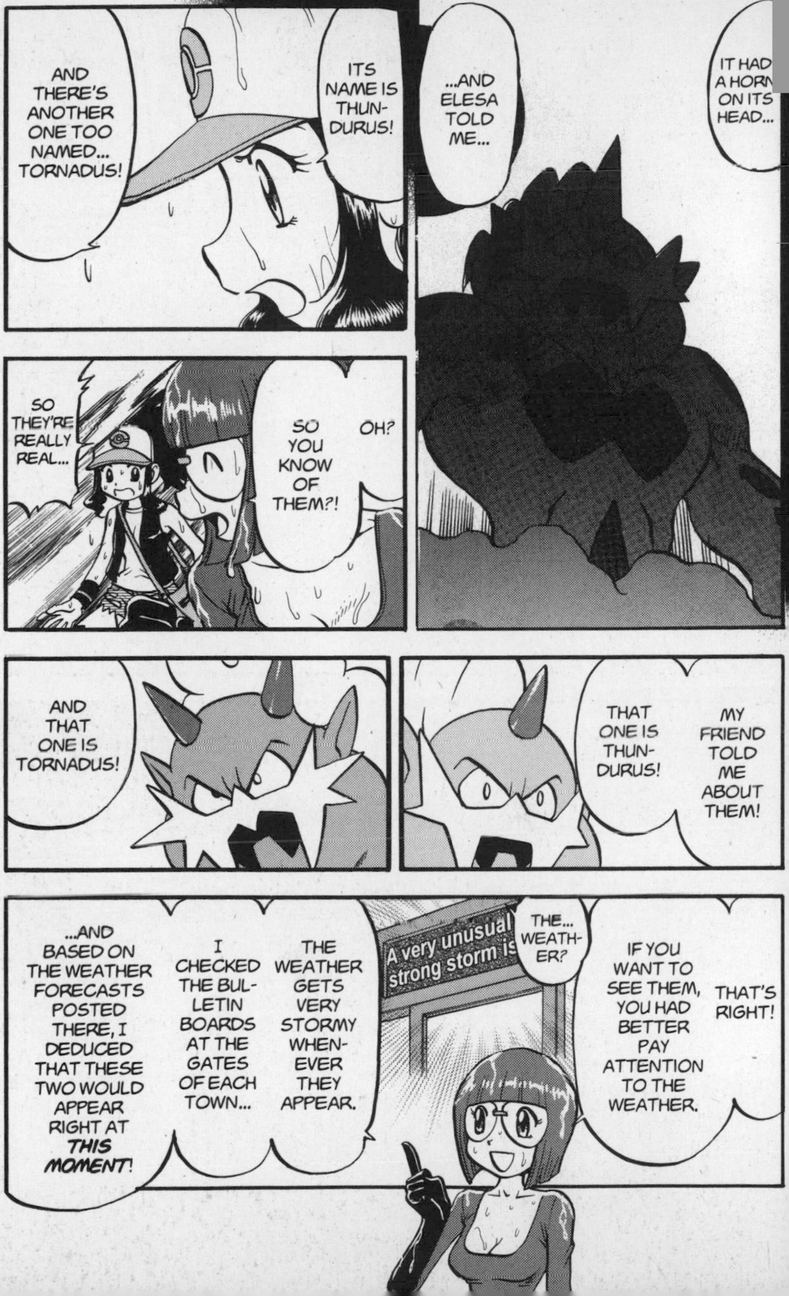
IT HAD A HORN ON ITS HEAD...
...AND ELESA TOLD ME...
ITS NAME IS THUN-DURUS!
AND THERE'S ANOTHER ONE TOO NAMED... TORNADUS!
OH?
SO YOU KNOW OF THEM?!
SO THEY'RE REALLY REAL...
MY FRIEND TOLD ME ABOUT THEM!
THAT ONE IS THUN-DURUS!
AND THAT ONE IS TORNADUS!
THAT'S RIGHT!
IF YOU WANT TO SEE THEM, YOU HAD BETTER PAY ATTENTION TO THE WEATHER.
THE... WEATHER?
A very unusual strong storm is
THE WEATHER GETS VERY STORMY WHEN-EVER THEY APPEAR.
I CHECKED THE BUL-LETIN BOARDS AT THE GATES OF EACH TOWN...
...AND BASED ON THE WEATHER FORECASTS POSTED THERE, I DEDUCED THAT THESE TWO WOULD APPEAR RIGHT AT ***THIS MOMENT***!

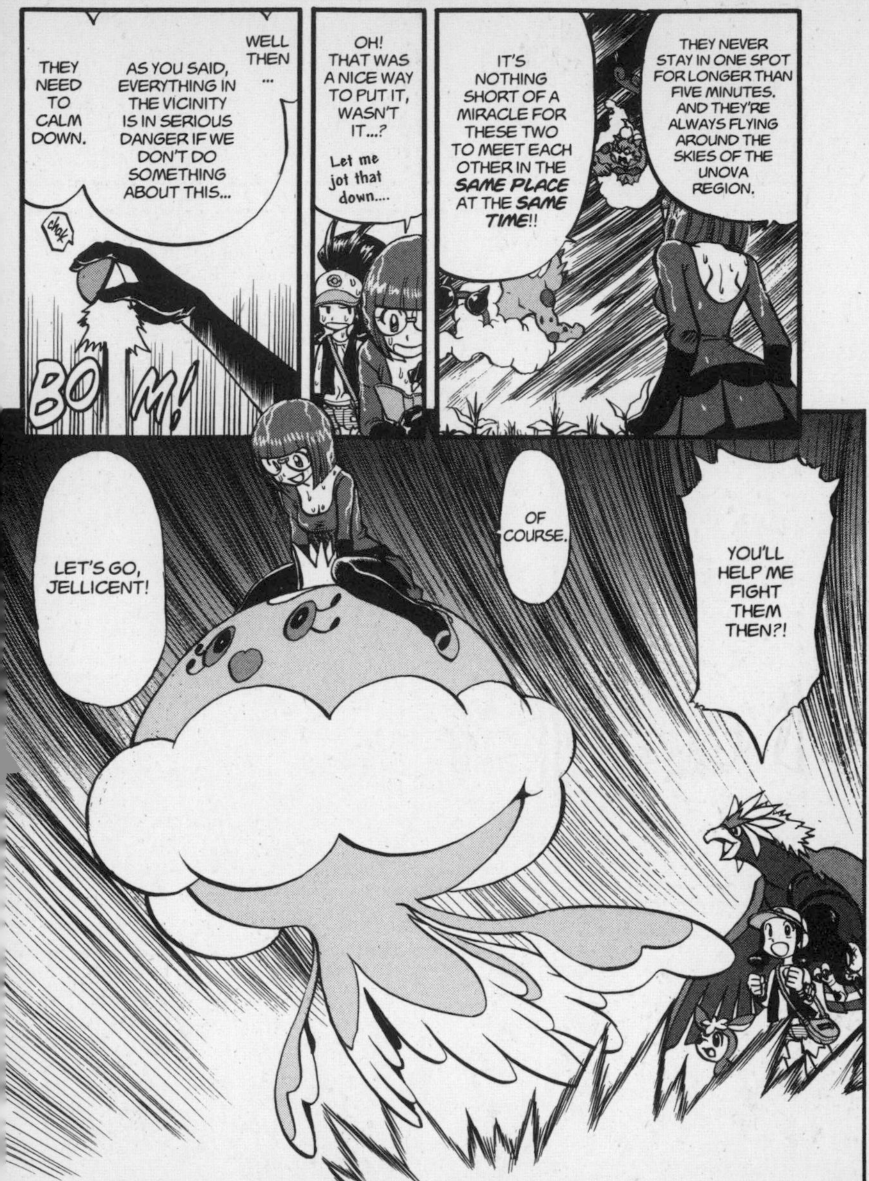
WELL THEN ...
AS YOU SAID, EVERYTHING IN THE VICINITY IS IN SERIOUS DANGER IF WE DON'T DO SOMETHING ABOUT THIS...
THEY NEED TO CALM DOWN.
chok
BOOM!
OH! THAT WAS A NICE WAY TO PUT IT, WASN'T IT...?
Let me jot that down....
THEY NEVER STAY IN ONE SPOT FOR LONGER THAN FIVE MINUTES. AND THEY'RE ALWAYS FLYING AROUND THE SKIES OF THE UNOVA REGION.
IT'S NOTHING SHORT OF A MIRACLE FOR THESE TWO TO MEET EACH OTHER IN THE SAME PLACE AT THE SAME TIME!!
YOU'LL HELP ME FIGHT THEM THEN?!
OF COURSE.
LET'S GO, JELLICENT!

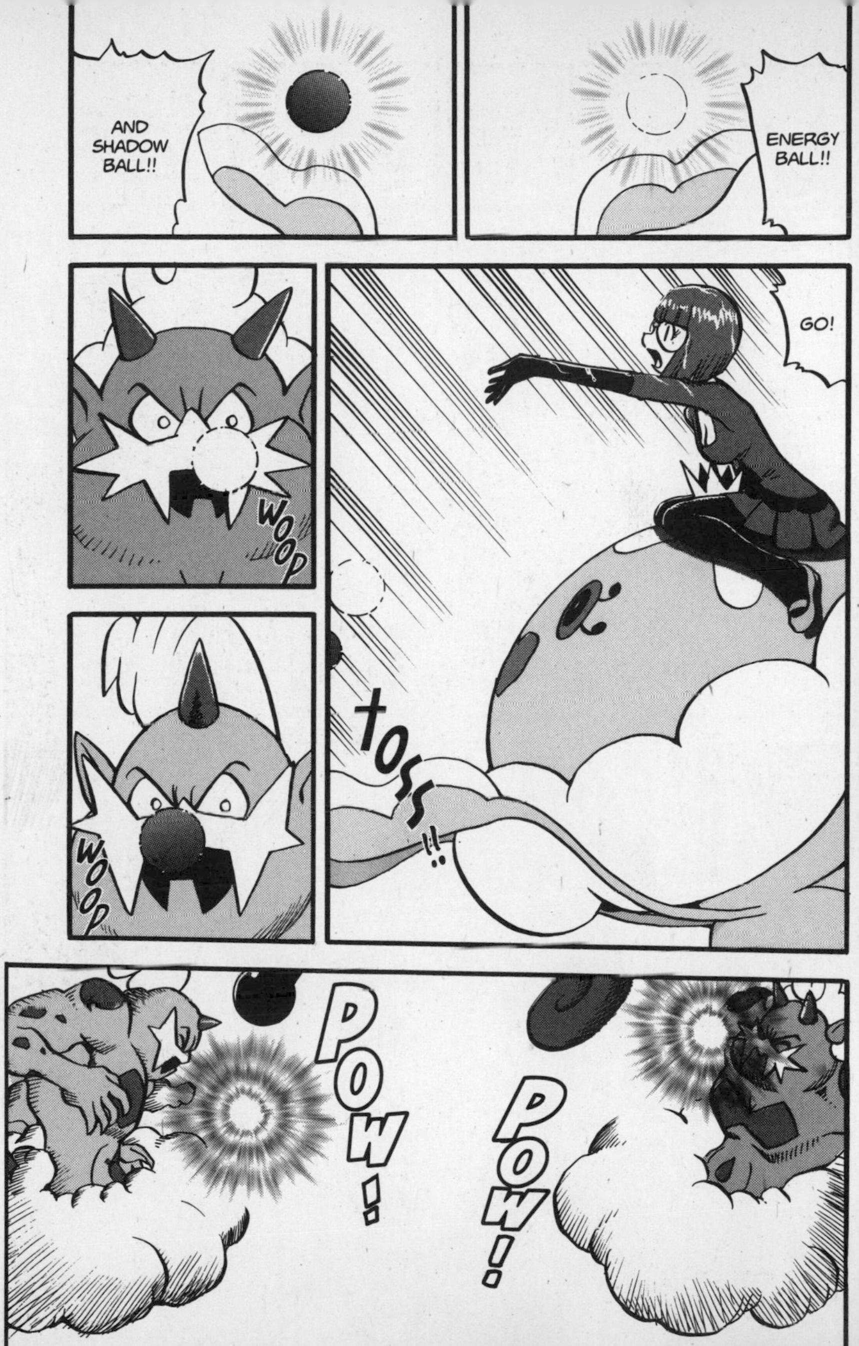
AND SHADOW BALL!!
ENERGY BALL!!
GO!
WOOP
WOOP
TOSS!!
POW!!
POW!!

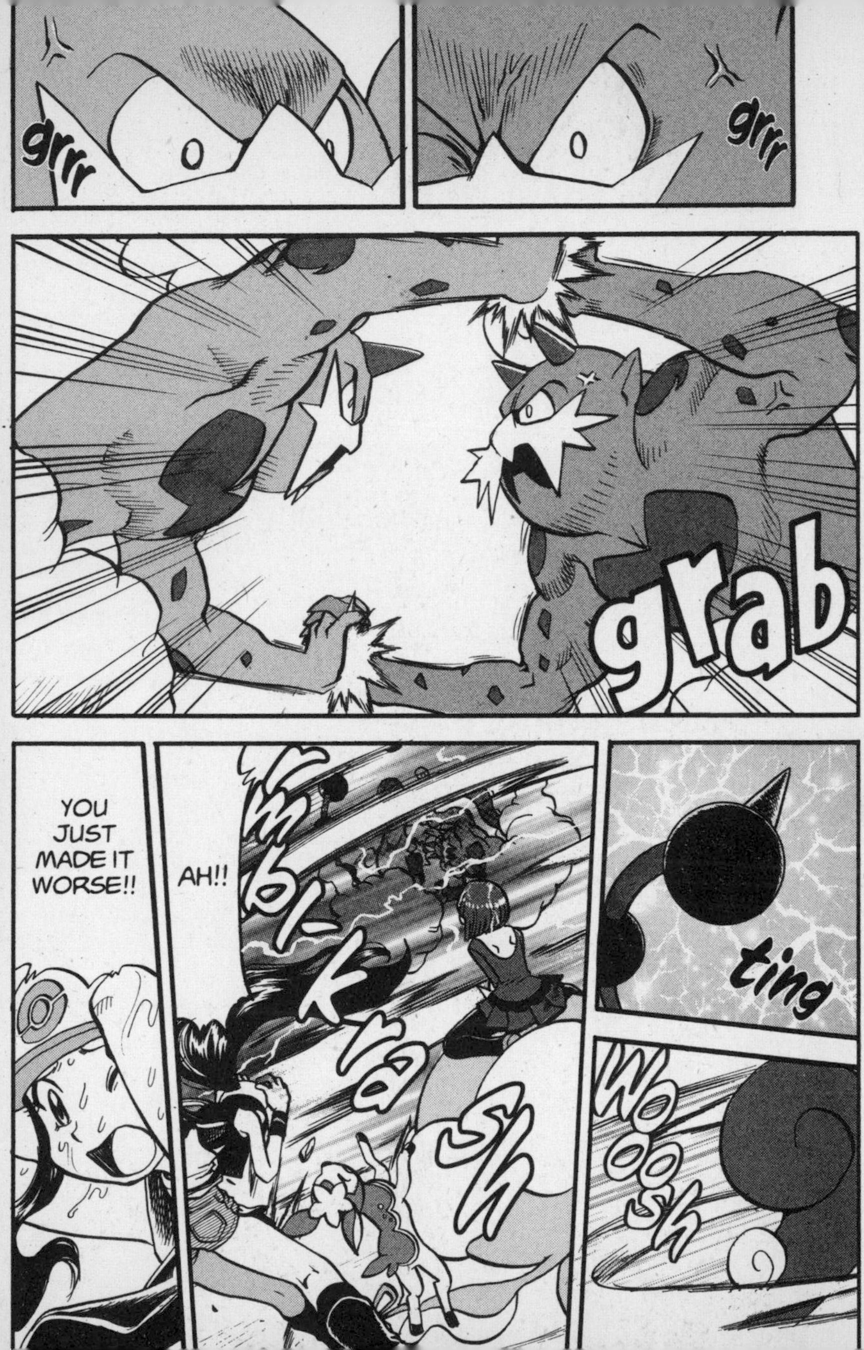
grrr
grrr
grab
YOU JUST MADE IT WORSE!!
AH!!
ting
whoosh

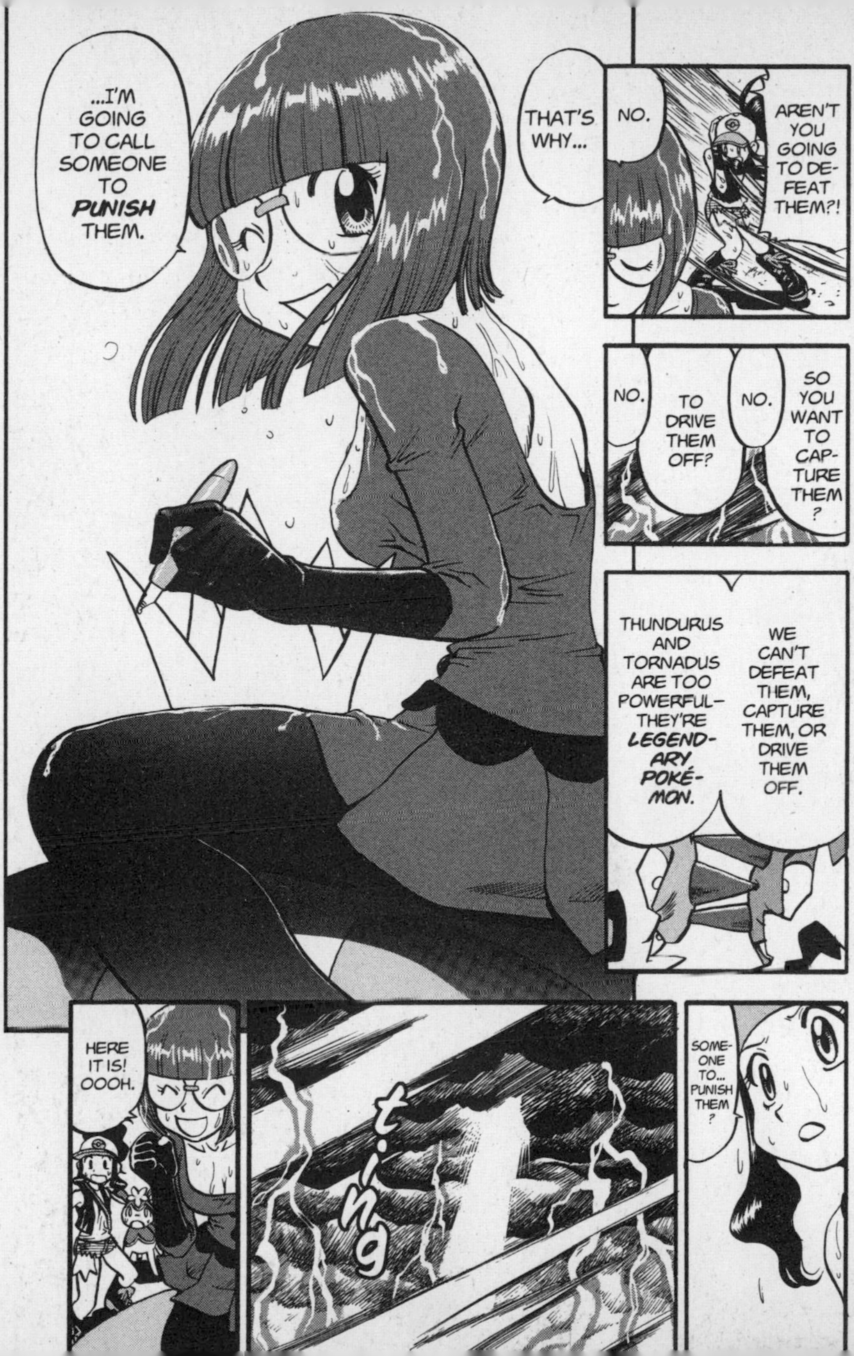

AREN'T YOU GOING TO DEFEAT THEM?!
NO.
SO YOU WANT TO CAPTURE THEM?
NO.
TO DRIVE THEM OFF?
NO.
WE CAN'T DEFEAT THEM, CAPTURE THEM, OR DRIVE THEM OFF.
THUNDURUS AND TORNADUS ARE TOO POWERFUL—THEY'RE LEGENDARY POKÉMON.
THAT'S WHY...
...I'M GOING TO CALL SOMEONE TO PUNISH THEM.
SOMEONE TO... PUNISH THEM?
ting
HERE IT IS! OOOH.

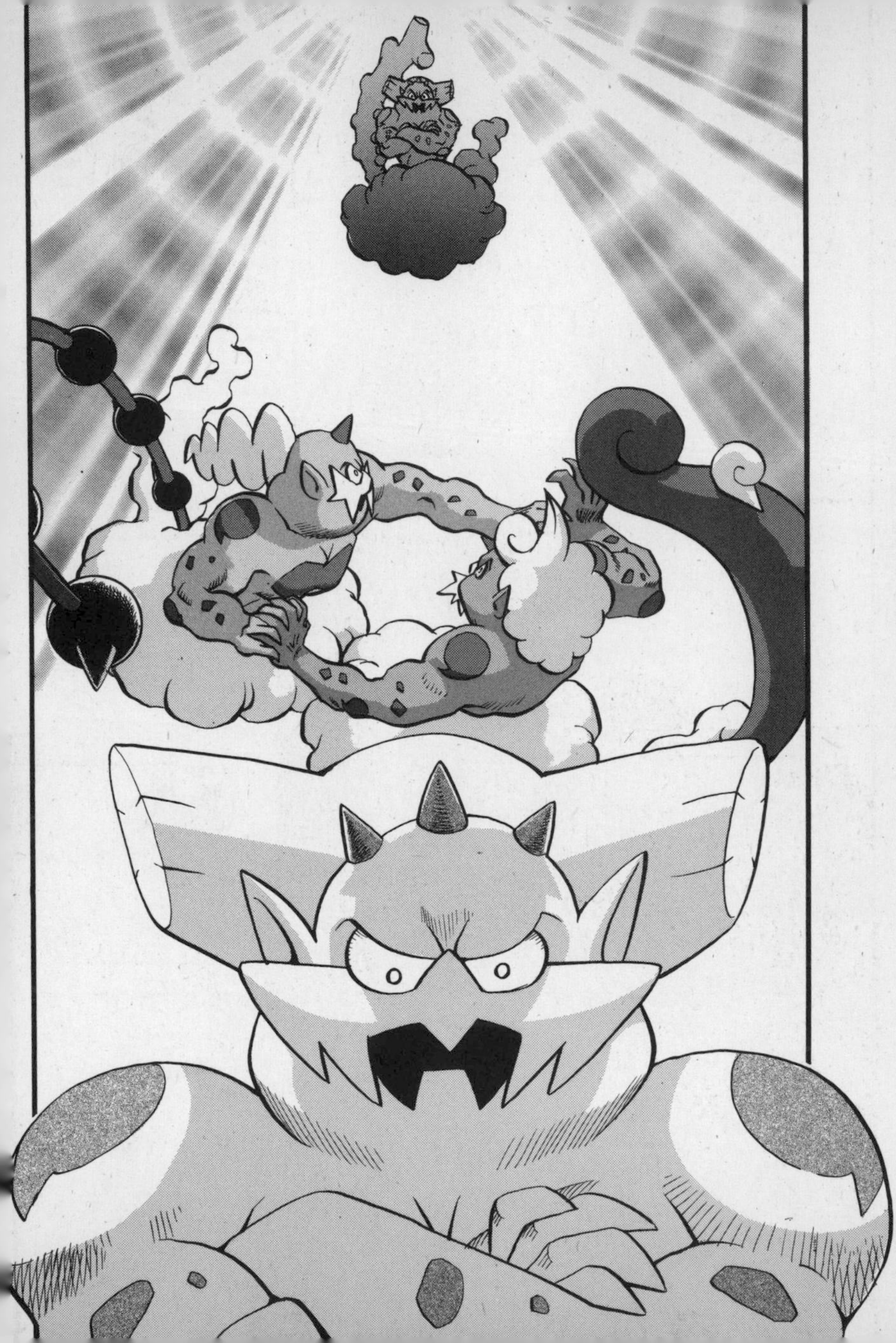

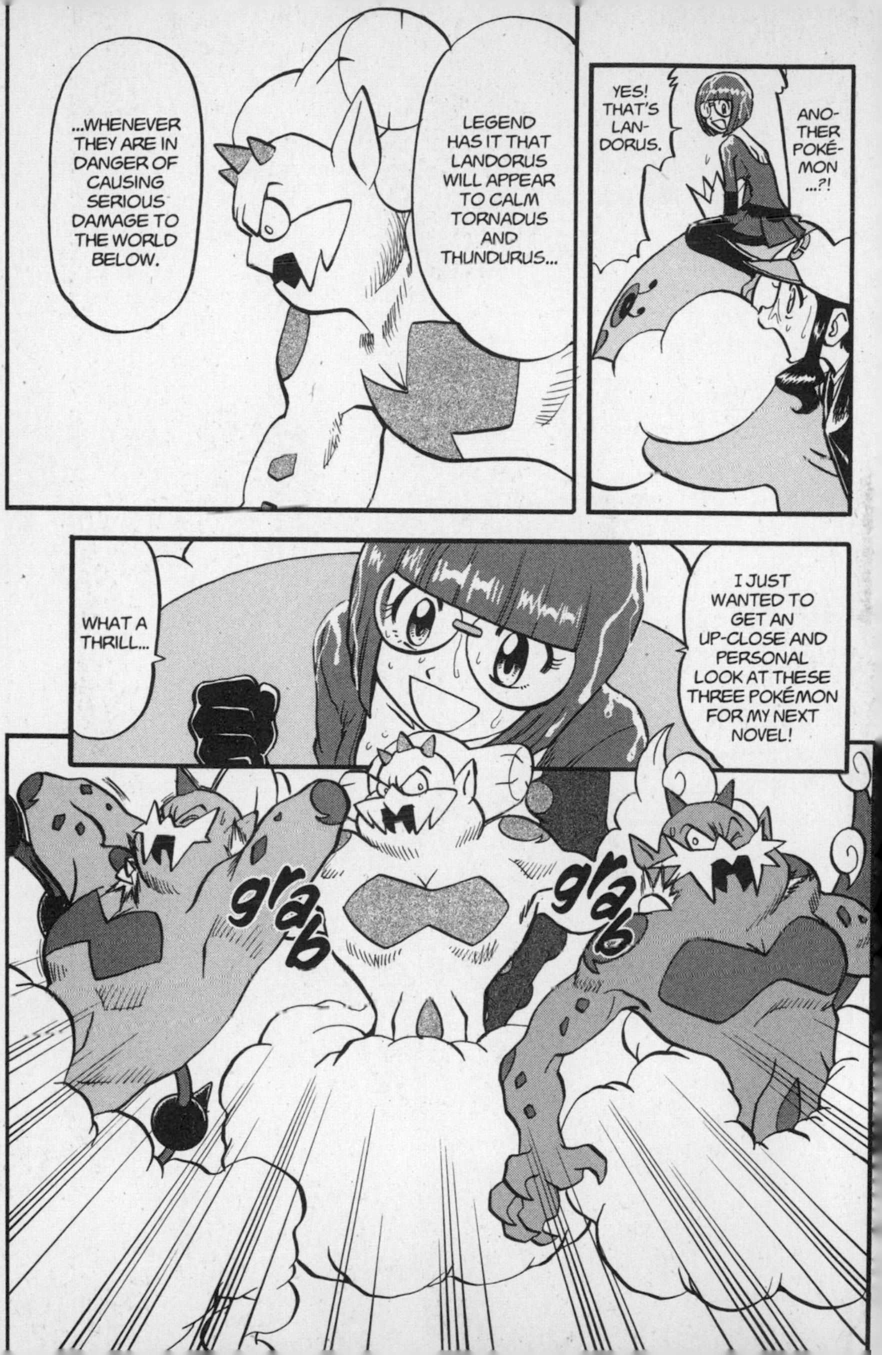
ANOTHER POKÉMON...?!
YES! THAT'S LANDORUS.
LEGEND HAS IT THAT LANDORUS WILL APPEAR TO CALM TORNADUS AND THUNDURUS...
...WHENEVER THEY ARE IN DANGER OF CAUSING SERIOUS DAMAGE TO THE WORLD BELOW.
I JUST WANTED TO GET AN UP-CLOSE AND PERSONAL LOOK AT THESE THREE POKÉMON FOR MY NEXT NOVEL!
WHAT A THRILL...
grab
grab

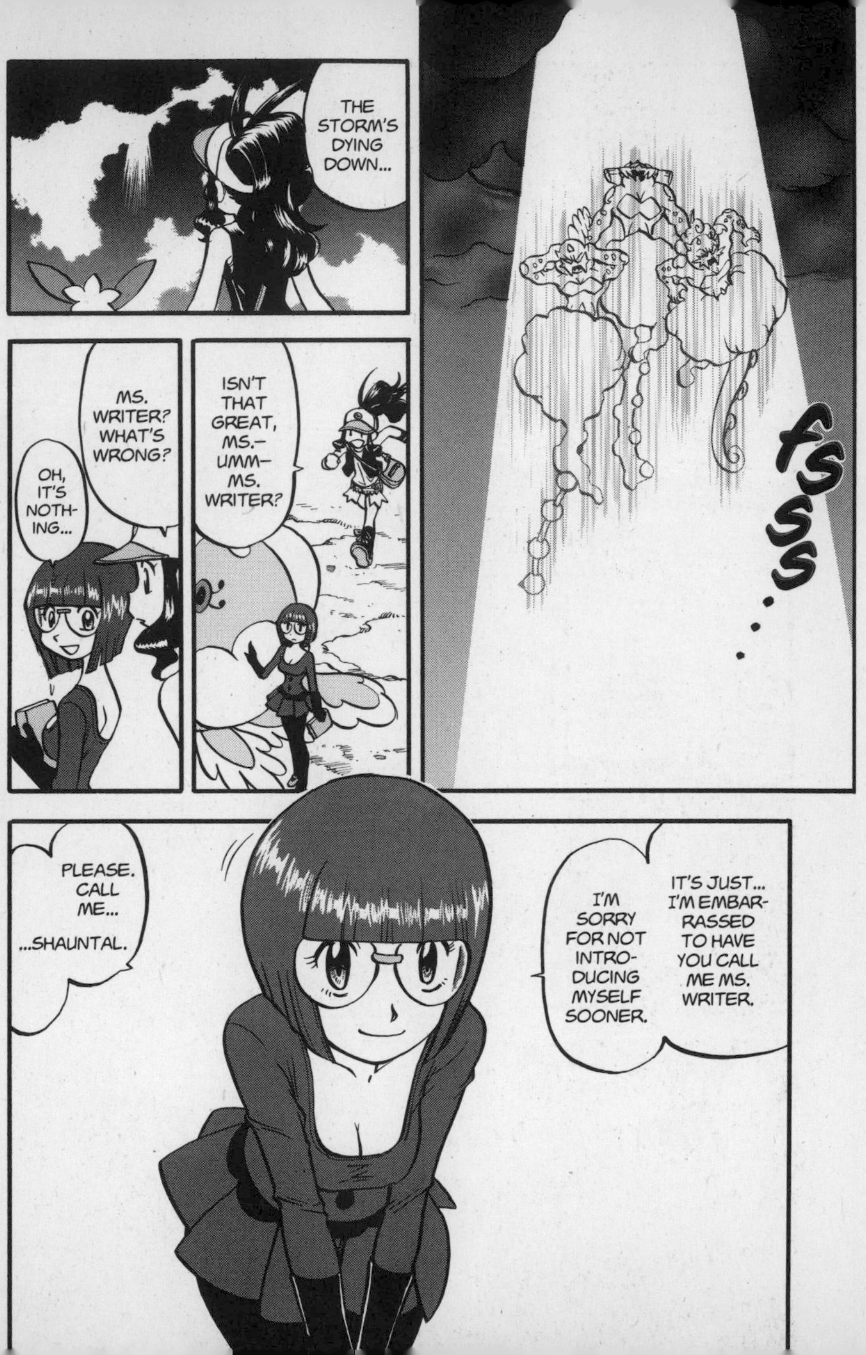
THE STORM'S DYING DOWN...
FSSSS...
ISN'T THAT GREAT, MS.– UMM– MS. WRITER?
MS. WRITER? WHAT'S WRONG?
OH, IT'S NOTH-ING...
IT'S JUST... I'M EMBAR-RASSED TO HAVE YOU CALL ME MS. WRITER.
I'M SORRY FOR NOT INTRO-DUCING MYSELF SOONER.
PLEASE. CALL ME...
...SHAUNTAL.

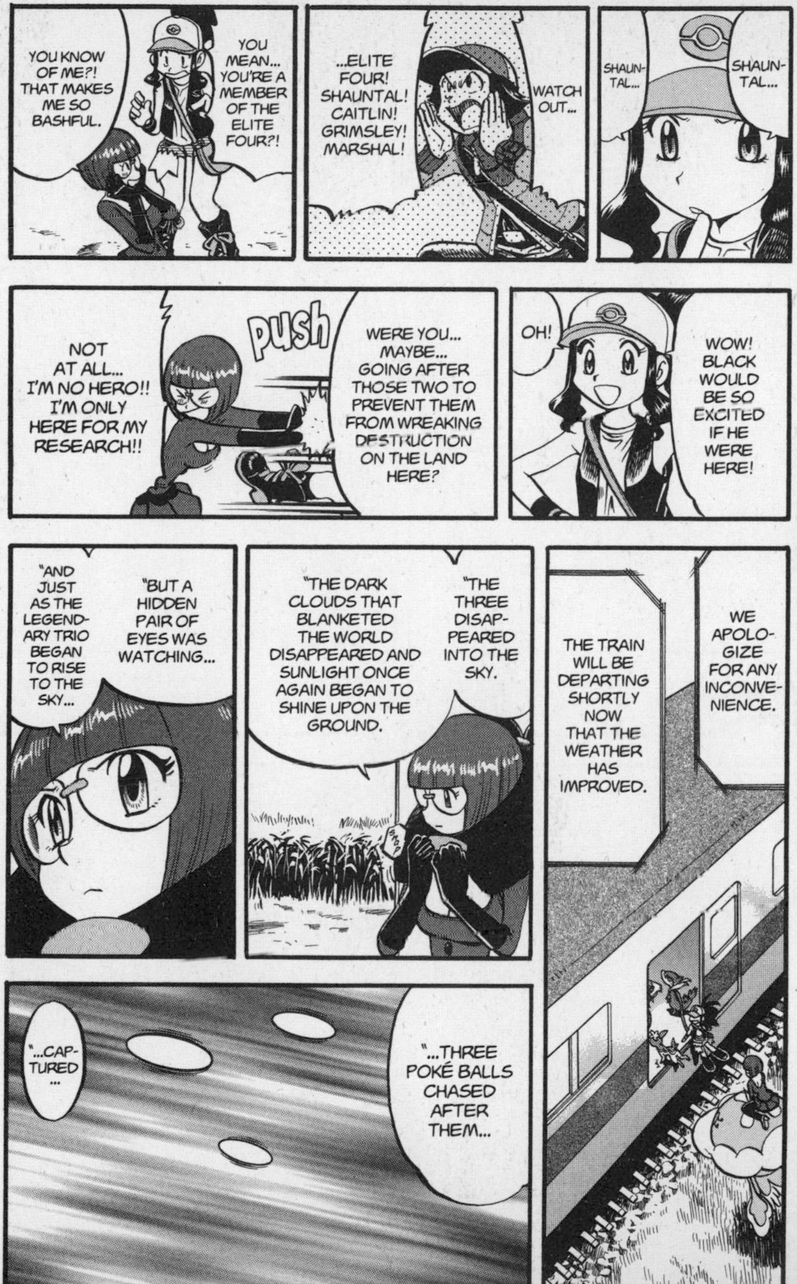

YOU KNOW OF ME?! THAT MAKES ME SO BASHFUL.
YOU MEAN... YOU'RE A MEMBER OF THE ELITE FOUR?!
...ELITE FOUR! SHAUNTAL! CAITLIN! GRIMSLEY! MARSHAL!
WATCH OUT...
SHAUN-TAL...
SHAUN-TAL...
NOT AT ALL... I'M NO HERO!! I'M ONLY HERE FOR MY RESEARCH!!
push
WERE YOU... MAYBE... GOING AFTER THOSE TWO TO PREVENT THEM FROM WREAKING DESTRUCTION ON THE LAND HERE?
OH!
WOW! BLACK WOULD BE SO EXCITED IF HE WERE HERE!
"AND JUST AS THE LEGEND-ARY TRIO BEGAN TO RISE TO THE SKY...
"BUT A HIDDEN PAIR OF EYES WAS WATCHING...
"THE DARK CLOUDS THAT BLANKETED THE WORLD DISAPPEARED AND SUNLIGHT ONCE AGAIN BEGAN TO SHINE UPON THE GROUND.
"THE THREE DISAP-PEARED INTO THE SKY.
THE TRAIN WILL BE DEPARTING SHORTLY NOW THAT THE WEATHER HAS IMPROVED.
WE APOLO-GIZE FOR ANY INCONVE-NIENCE.
"...CAP-TURED ...
"...THREE POKÉ BALLS CHASED AFTER THEM...

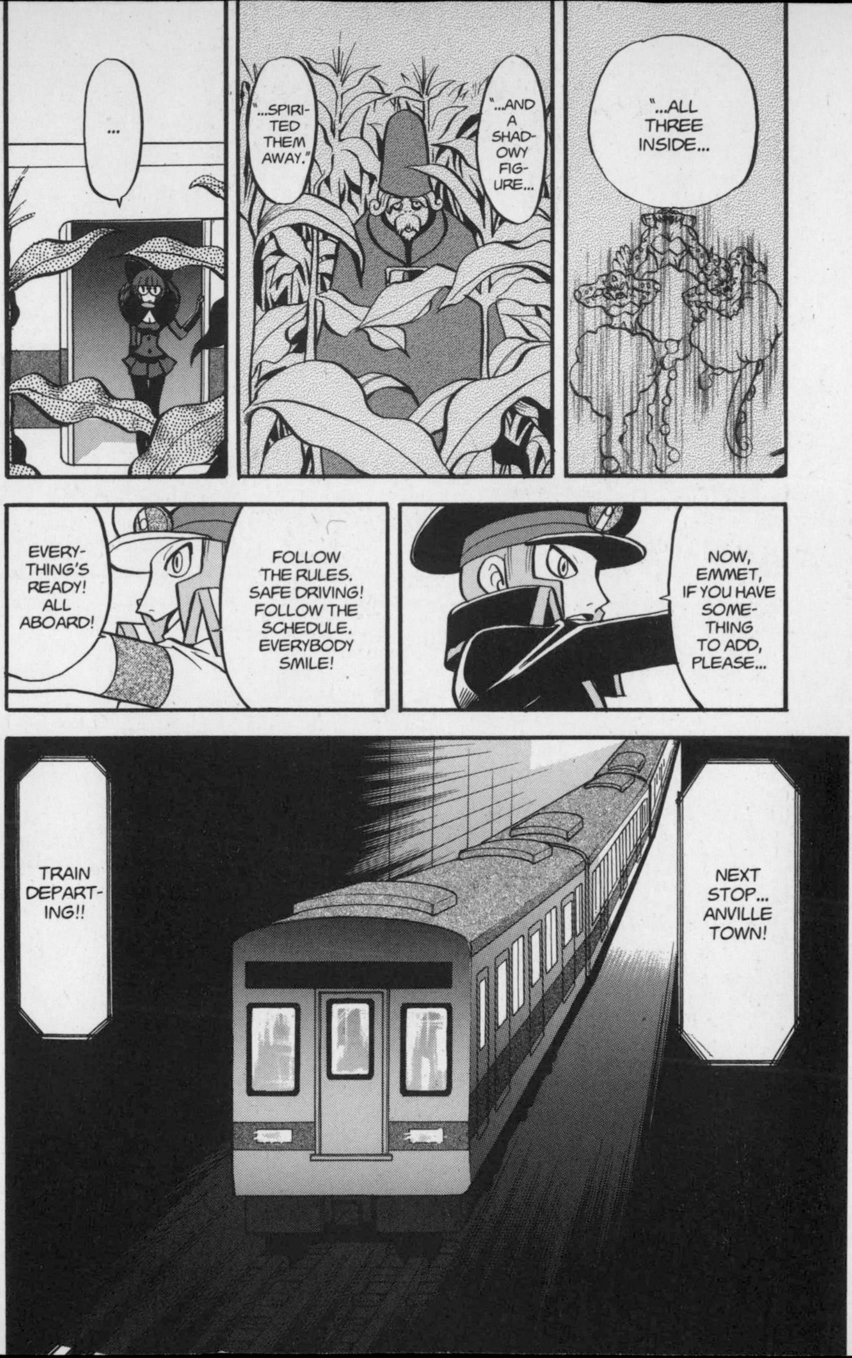
"...ALL THREE INSIDE...
"...AND A SHADOWY FIGURE...
"...SPIRITED THEM AWAY."
...
NOW, EMMET, IF YOU HAVE SOMETHING TO ADD, PLEASE...
FOLLOW THE RULES. SAFE DRIVING! FOLLOW THE SCHEDULE. EVERYBODY SMILE!
EVERYTHING'S READY! ALL ABOARD!
NEXT STOP... ANVILLE TOWN!
TRAIN DEPARTING!!

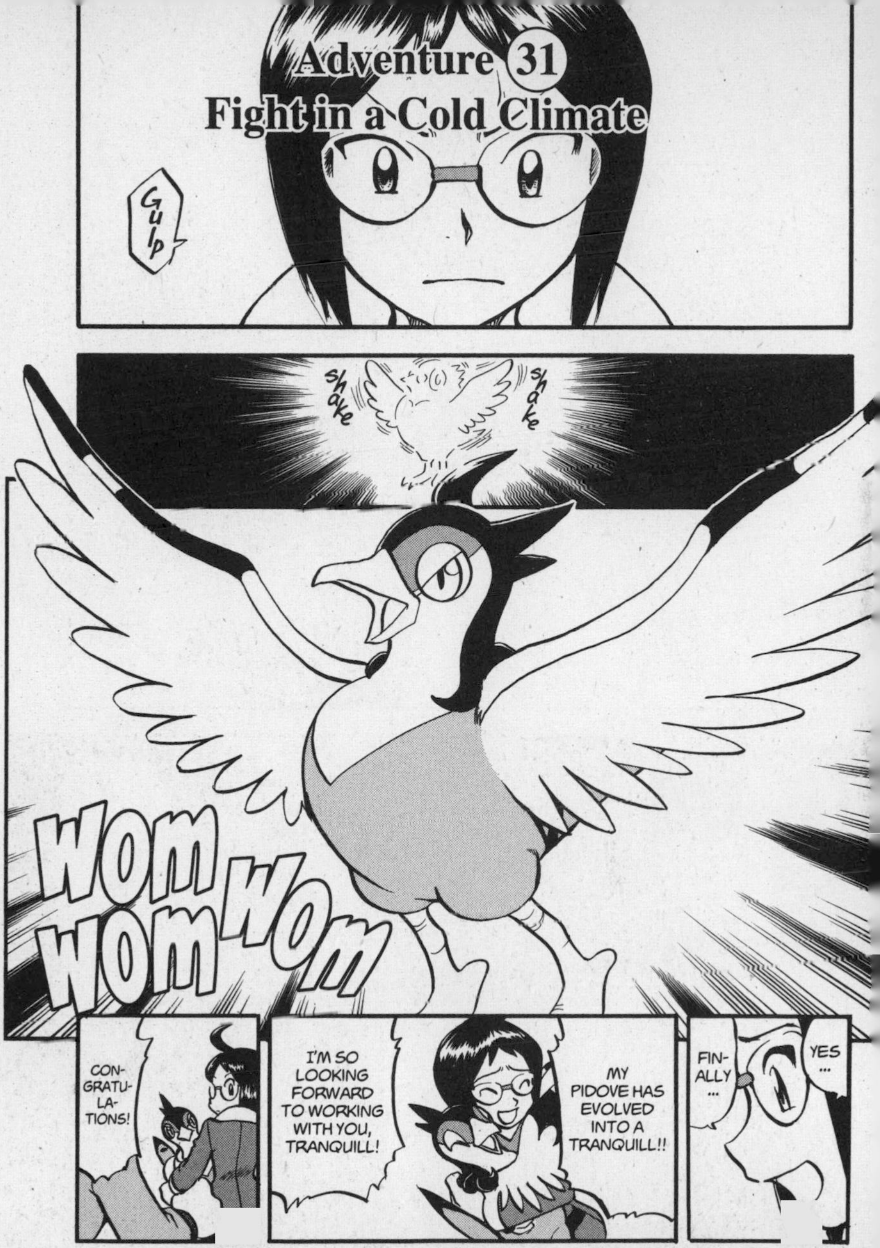
Adventure 31
Fight in a Cold Climate
Gulp
shake
shake
WOM WOM
WOM WOM
YES ...
FIN-ALLY ...
MY PIDOVE HAS EVOLVED INTO A TRANQUILL!!
I'M SO LOOKING FORWARD TO WORKING WITH YOU, TRANQUILL!
CON-GRATU-LA-TIONS!

Adventure 31
Fight in a Cold Climate

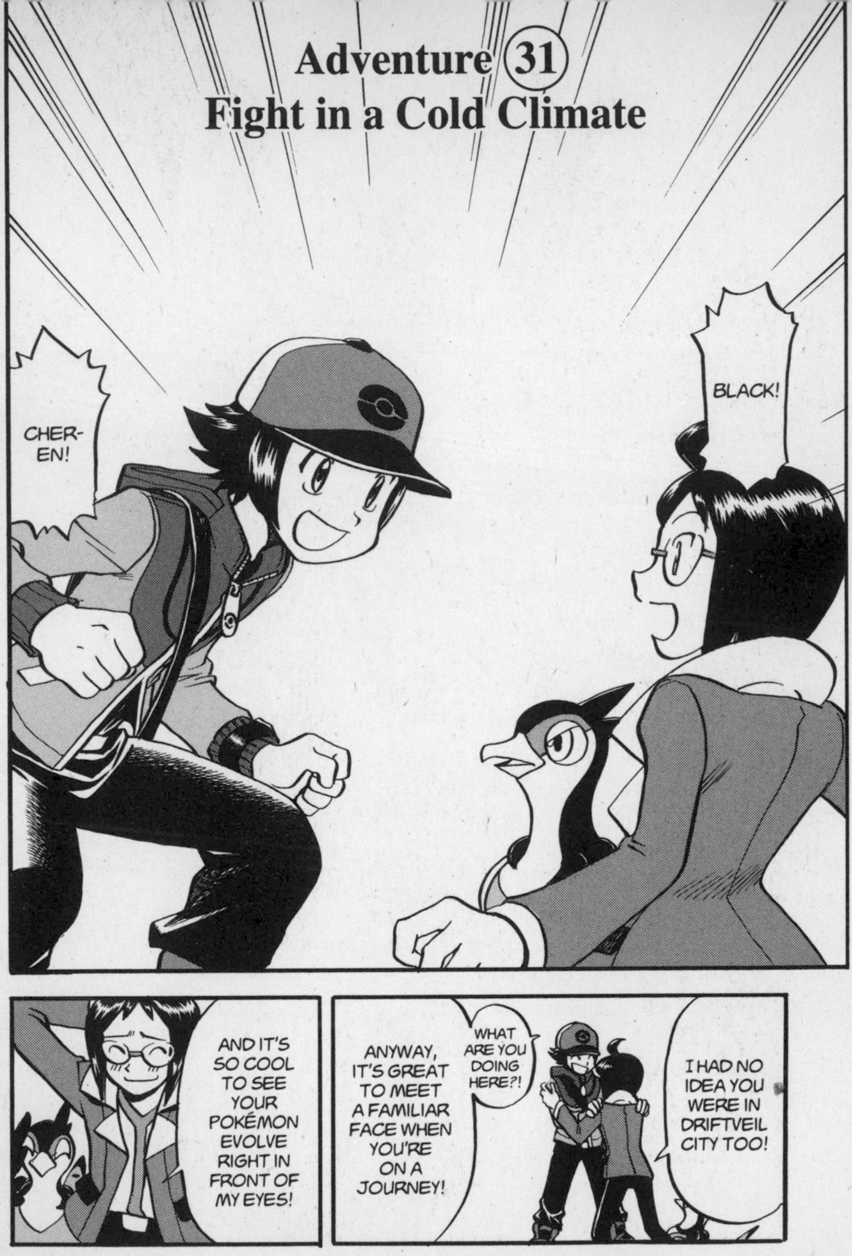
CHER-EN!
BLACK!
AND IT'S SO COOL TO SEE YOUR POKÉMON EVOLVE RIGHT IN FRONT OF MY EYES!
ANYWAY, IT'S GREAT TO MEET A FAMILIAR FACE WHEN YOU'RE ON A JOURNEY!
WHAT ARE YOU DOING HERE?!
I HAD NO IDEA YOU WERE IN DRIFTVEIL CITY TOO!

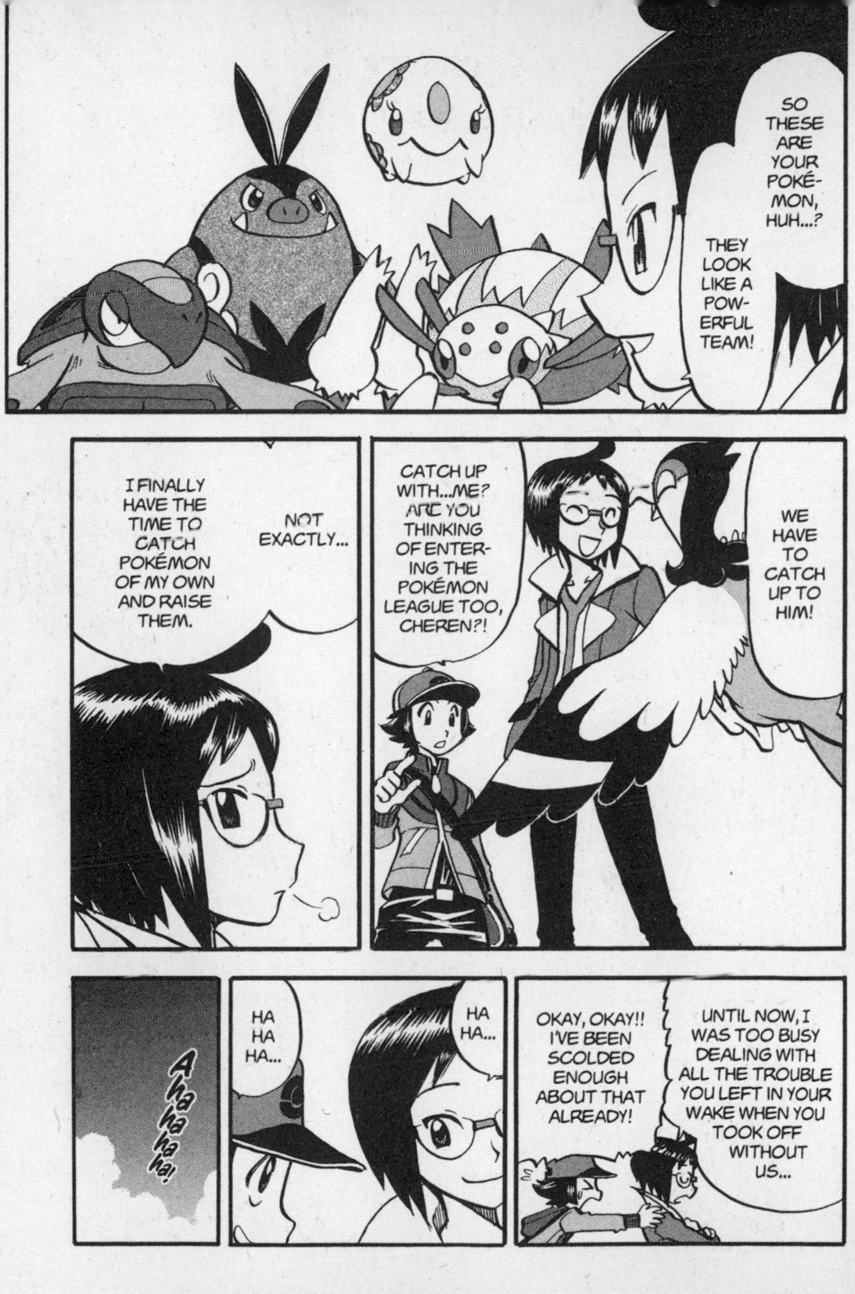
SO THESE ARE YOUR POKÉMON, HUH...?
THEY LOOK LIKE A POWERFUL TEAM!
WE HAVE TO CATCH UP TO HIM!
CATCH UP WITH...ME? ARE YOU THINKING OF ENTERING THE POKÉMON LEAGUE TOO, CHEREN?!
NOT EXACTLY...
I FINALLY HAVE THE TIME TO CATCH POKÉMON OF MY OWN AND RAISE THEM.
UNTIL NOW, I WAS TOO BUSY DEALING WITH ALL THE TROUBLE YOU LEFT IN YOUR WAKE WHEN YOU TOOK OFF WITHOUT US...
OKAY, OKAY!! I'VE BEEN SCOLDED ENOUGH ABOUT THAT ALREADY!
HA HA...
HA HA HA...
Ahahahaha!

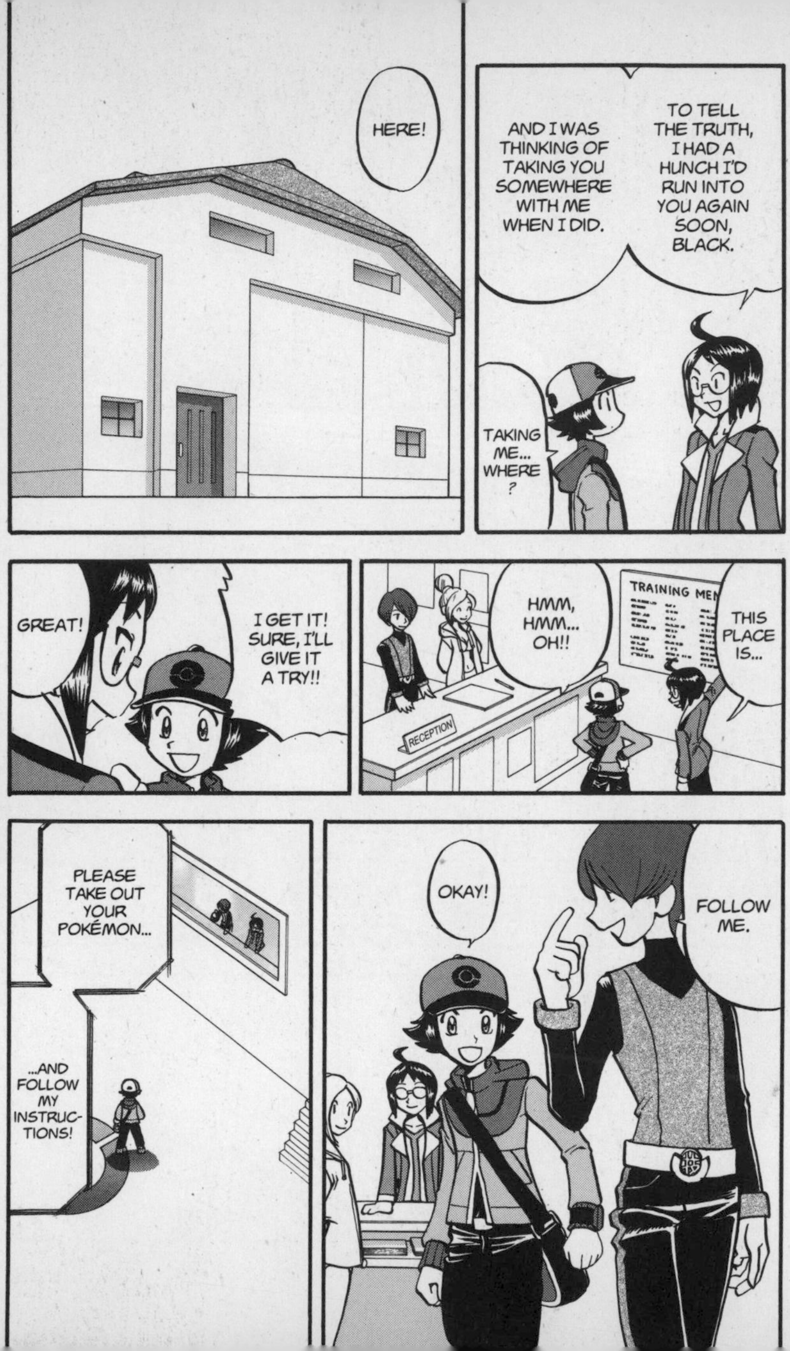

HERE!
TO TELL THE TRUTH, I HAD A HUNCH I'D RUN INTO YOU AGAIN SOON, BLACK.
AND I WAS THINKING OF TAKING YOU SOMEWHERE WITH ME WHEN I DID.
TAKING ME... WHERE?
GREAT!
I GET IT! SURE, I'LL GIVE IT A TRY!!
HMM, HMM... OH!!
TRAINING MEN
THIS PLACE IS...
RECEPTION
PLEASE TAKE OUT YOUR POKÉMON...
...AND FOLLOW MY INSTRUCTIONS!
OKAY!
FOLLOW ME.

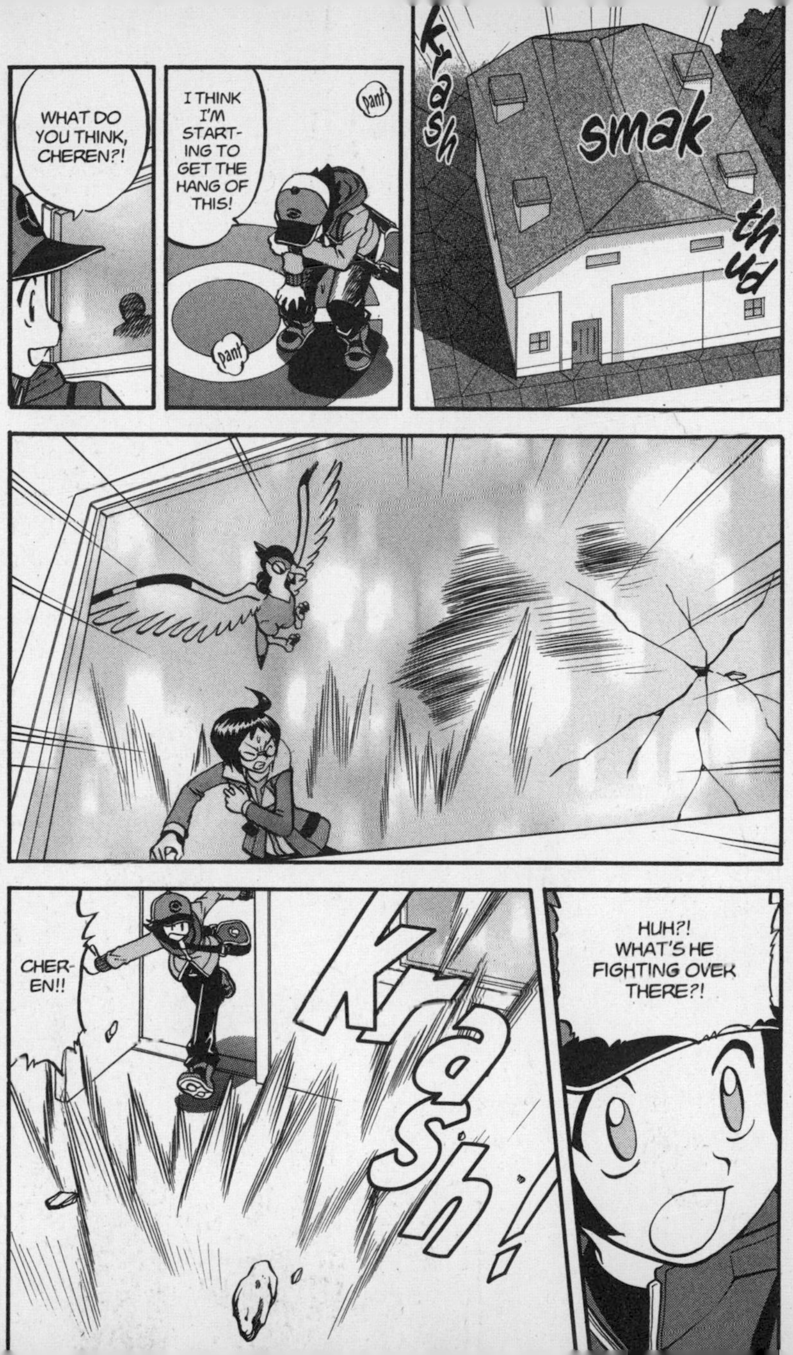

WHAT DO YOU THINK, CHEREN?!
I THINK I'M STARTING TO GET THE HANG OF THIS!
pant
pant
krash
smak
thud
CHER-EN!!
Krash!
HUH?! WHAT'S HE FIGHTING OVER THERE?!

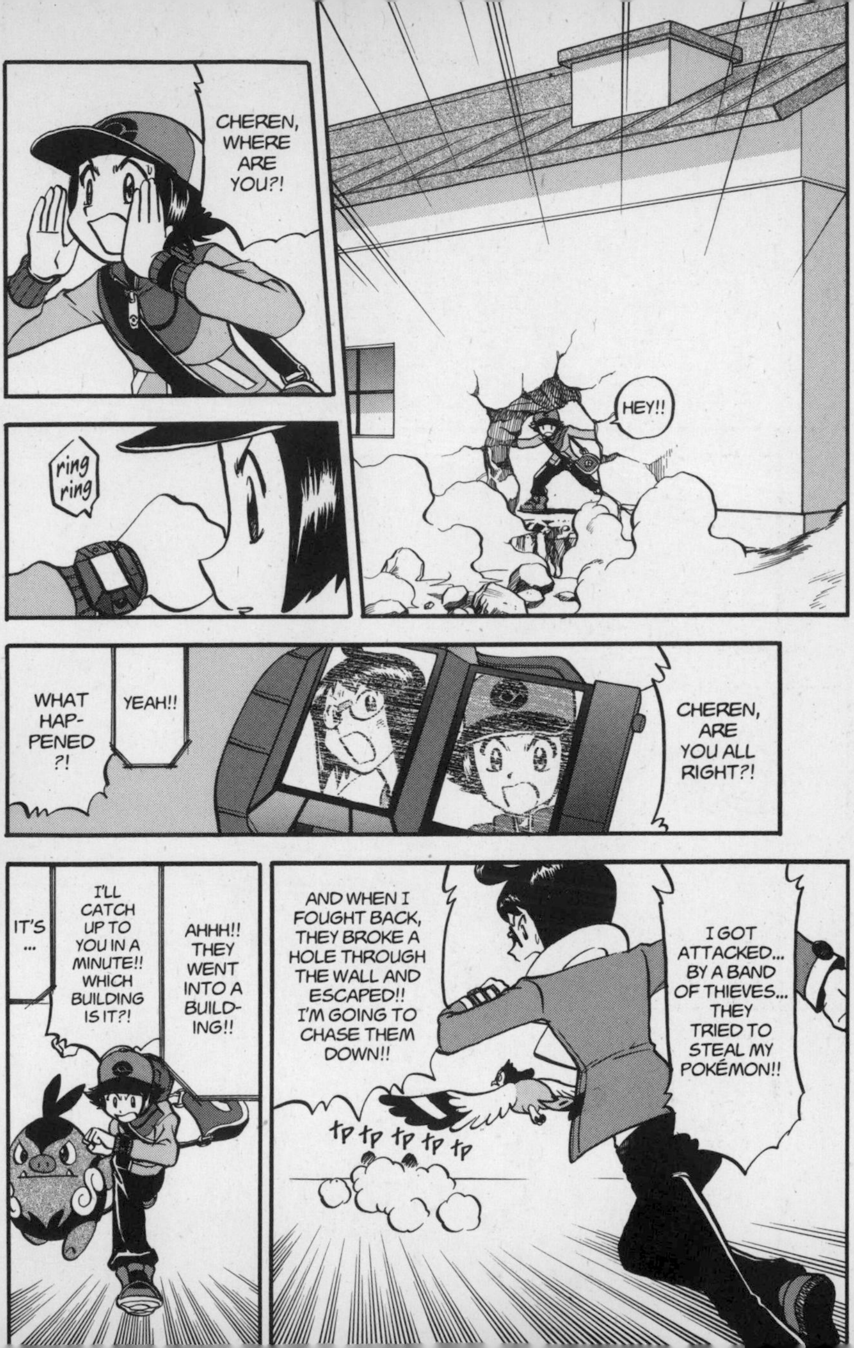
CHEREN, WHERE ARE YOU?!
ring ring
HEY!!
CHEREN, ARE YOU ALL RIGHT?!
YEAH!!
WHAT HAP-PENED ?!
I GOT ATTACKED... BY A BAND OF THIEVES... THEY TRIED TO STEAL MY POKÉMON!!
AND WHEN I FOUGHT BACK, THEY BROKE A HOLE THROUGH THE WALL AND ESCAPED!! I'M GOING TO CHASE THEM DOWN!!
tp tp tp tp tp
AHHH!! THEY WENT INTO A BUILD-ING!!
I'LL CATCH UP TO YOU IN A MINUTE!! WHICH BUILDING IS IT?!
IT'S ...

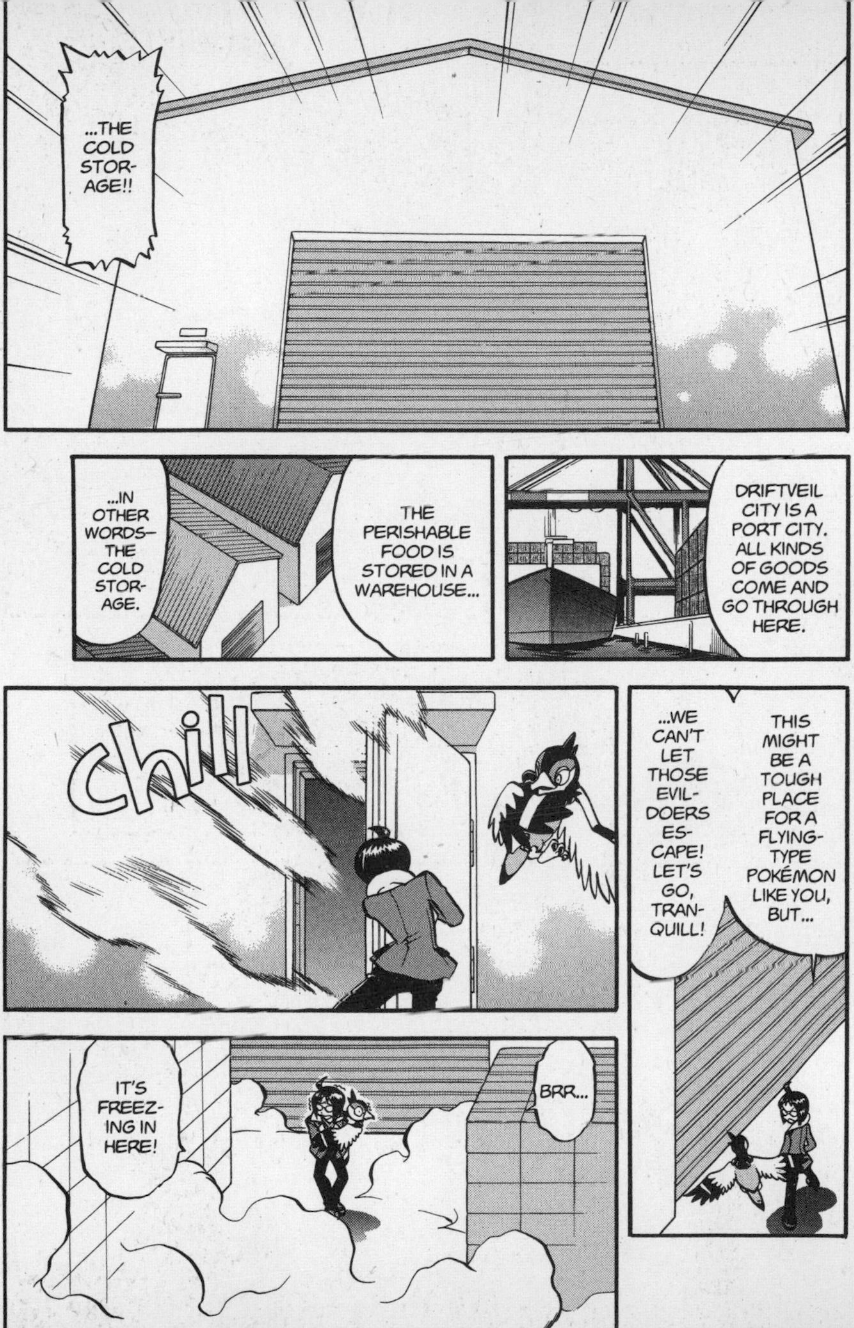
...THE COLD STOR-AGE!!
DRIFTVEIL CITY IS A PORT CITY. ALL KINDS OF GOODS COME AND GO THROUGH HERE.
THE PERISHABLE FOOD IS STORED IN A WAREHOUSE...
...IN OTHER WORDS—THE COLD STOR-AGE.
THIS MIGHT BE A TOUGH PLACE FOR A FLYING-TYPE POKÉMON LIKE YOU, BUT...
...WE CAN'T LET THOSE EVIL-DOERS ES-CAPE! LET'S GO, TRAN-QUILL!
Chill
BRR...
IT'S FREEZ-ING IN HERE!

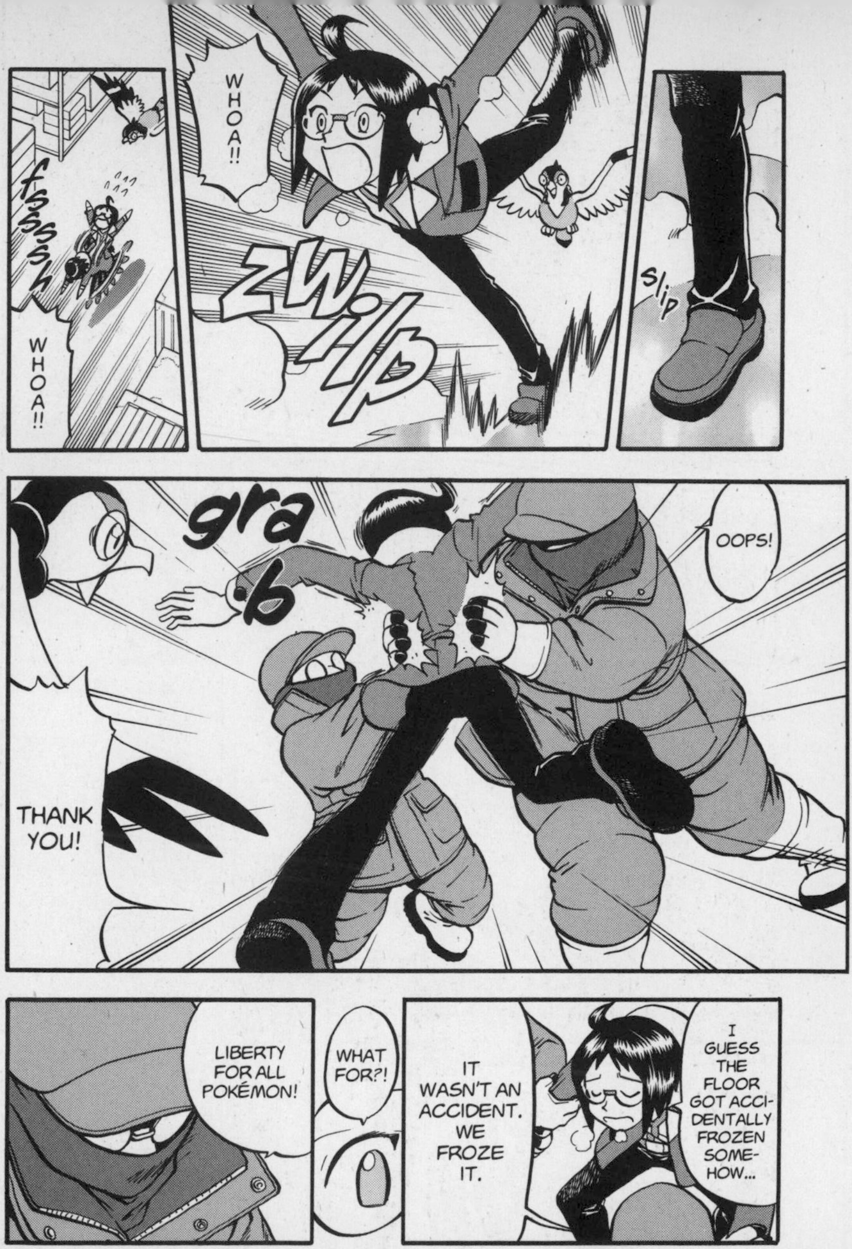
fsssh
WHOA!!
WHOA!!
zwilp
slip
grab
OOPS!
THANK YOU!
LIBERTY FOR ALL POKÉMON!
WHAT FOR?!
IT WASN'T AN ACCIDENT. WE FROZE IT.
I GUESS THE FLOOR GOT ACCI-DENTALLY FROZEN SOME-HOW...

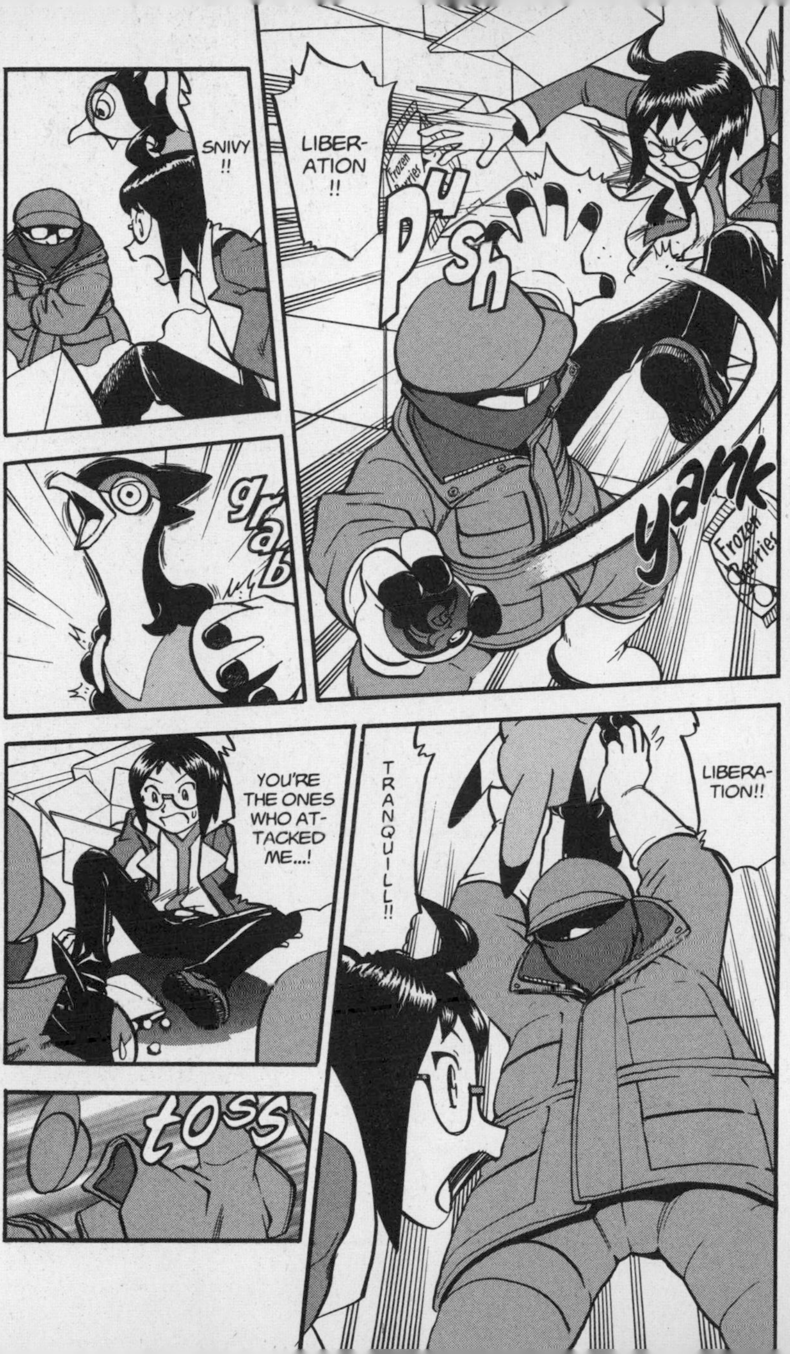
SNIVY !!
LIBERATION !!
Frozen Berries
push
grab
yank
Frozen Berries
YOU'RE THE ONES WHO ATTACKED ME...!
TRANQUILL!!
LIBERATION!!
toss

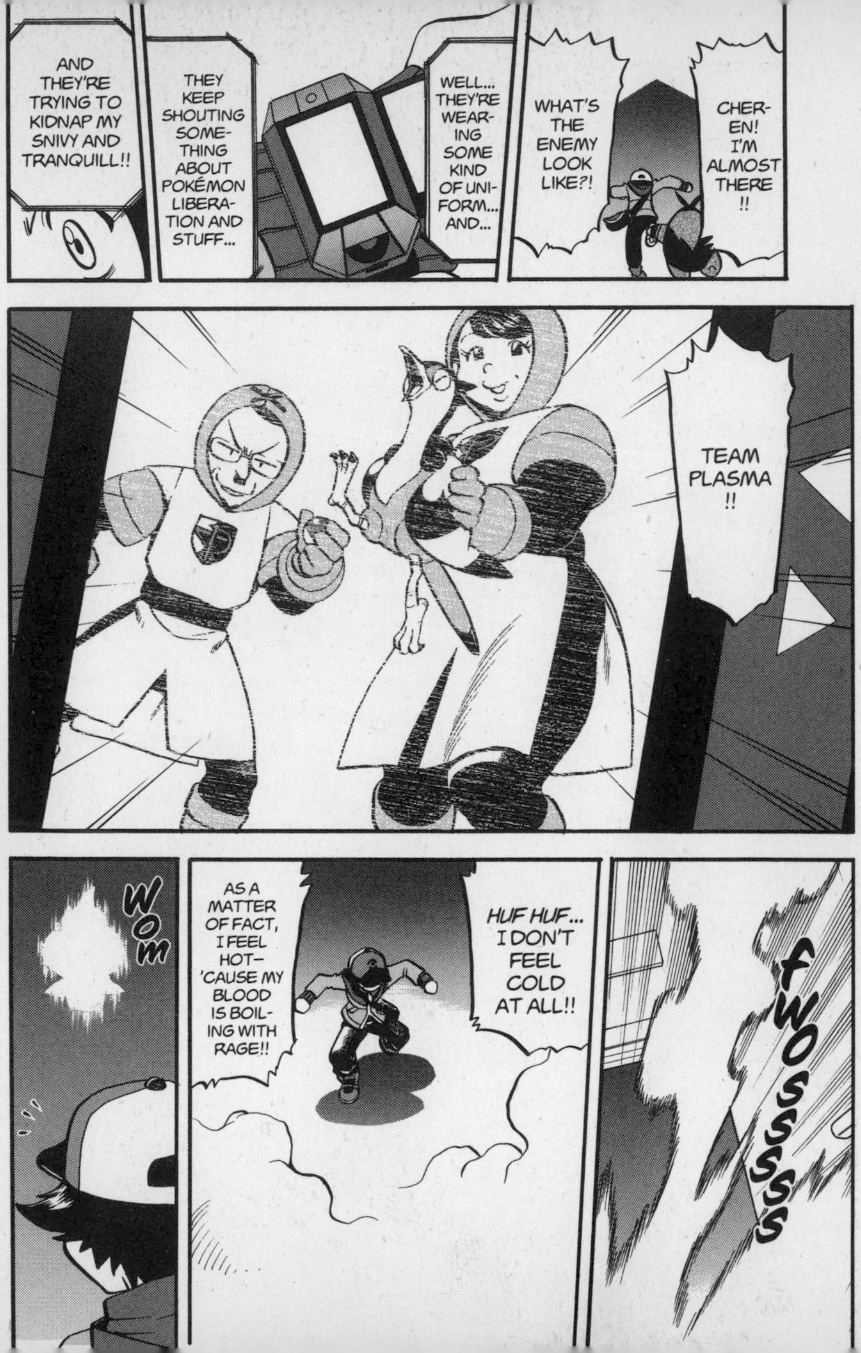
CHEREN! I'M ALMOST THERE!!
WHAT'S THE ENEMY LOOK LIKE?!
WELL... THEY'RE WEARING SOME KIND OF UNIFORM... AND...
THEY KEEP SHOUTING SOMETHING ABOUT POKÉMON LIBERATION AND STUFF...
AND THEY'RE TRYING TO KIDNAP MY SNIVY AND TRANQUILL!!
TEAM PLASMA!!
FWOSSSSS
HUF HUF... I DON'T FEEL COLD AT ALL!!
AS A MATTER OF FACT, I FEEL HOT—'CAUSE MY BLOOD IS BOILING WITH RAGE!!
WOM

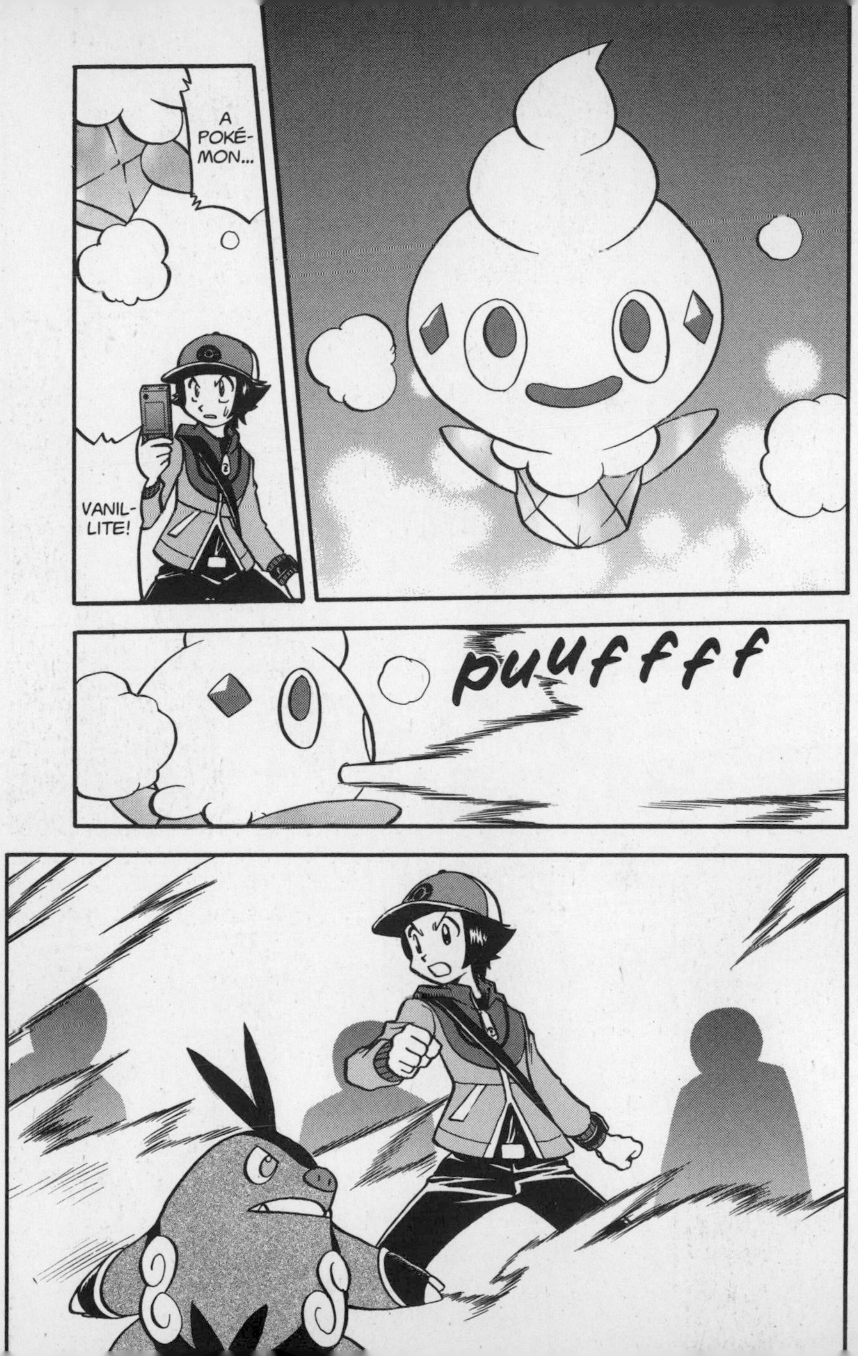
A POKÉ-MON...
VANIL-LITE!
puuffff

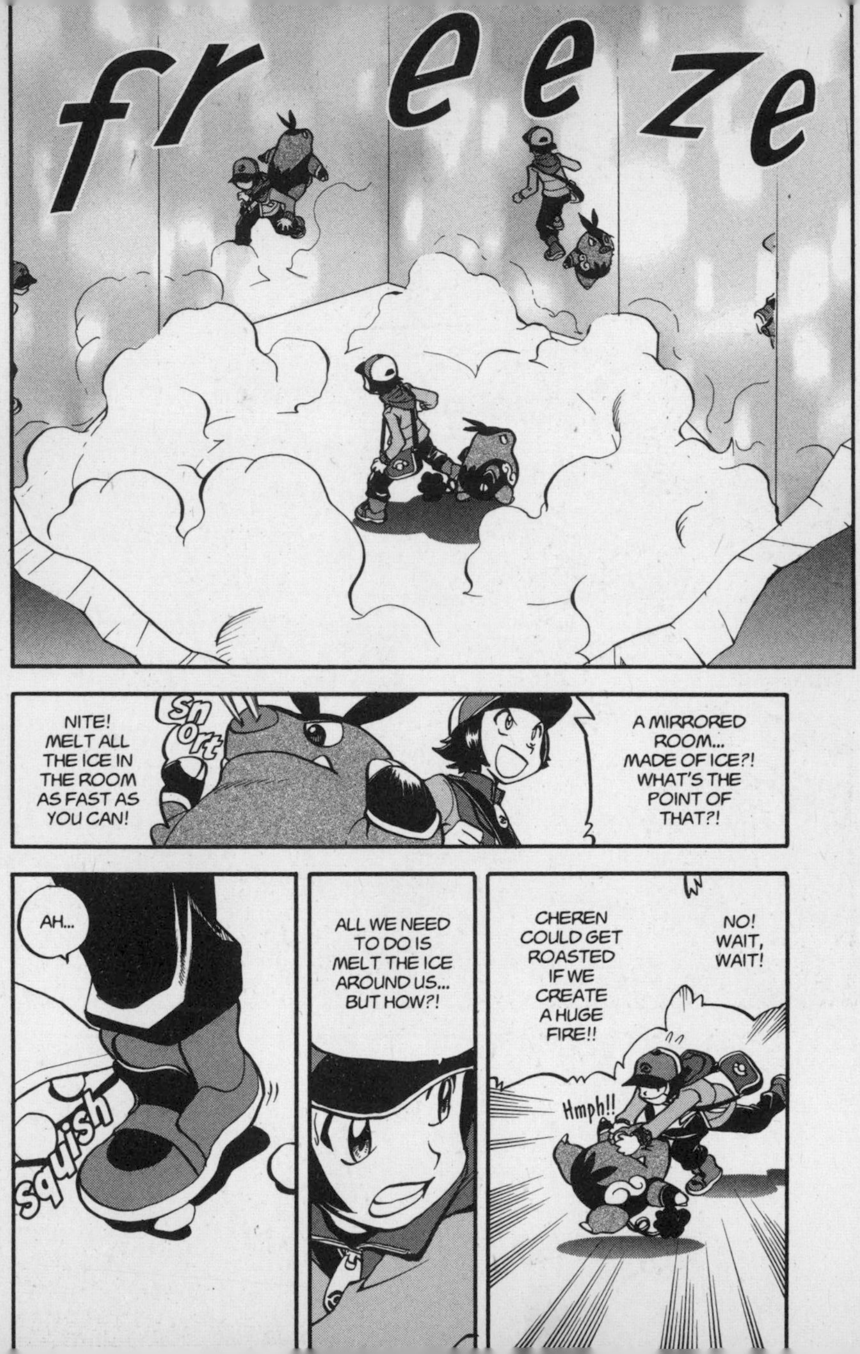
freeze
A MIRRORED ROOM... MADE OF ICE?! WHAT'S THE POINT OF THAT?!
snort
NITE! MELT ALL THE ICE IN THE ROOM AS FAST AS YOU CAN!
AH...
squish
ALL WE NEED TO DO IS MELT THE ICE AROUND US... BUT HOW?!
NO! WAIT, WAIT!
CHEREN COULD GET ROASTED IF WE CREATE A HUGE FIRE!!
Hmph!!

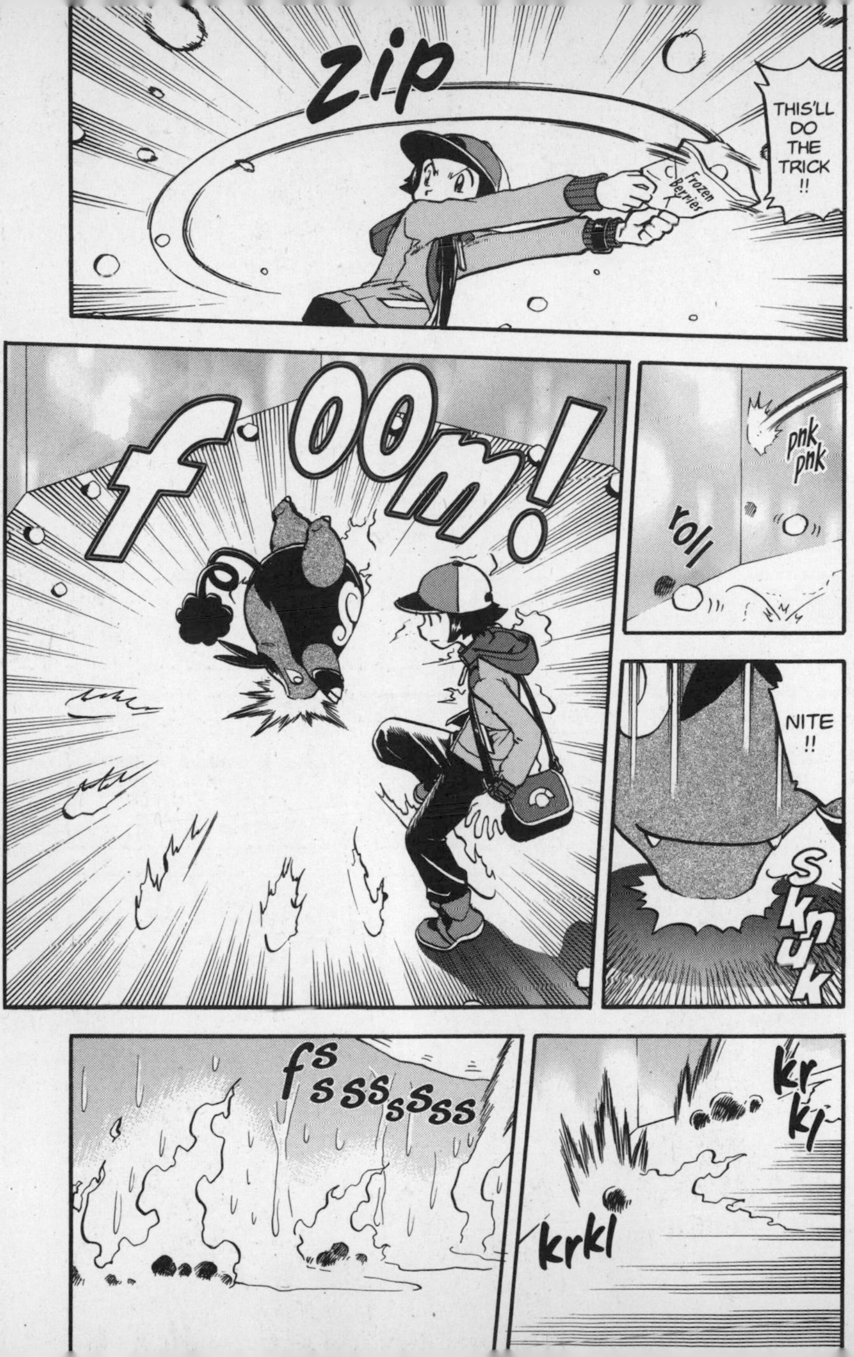
zip
THIS'LL DO THE TRICK !!
Frozen Berries
fOOm!
pnk pnk
roll
NITE !!
Sknuk
fsssssss
krkl
krkl

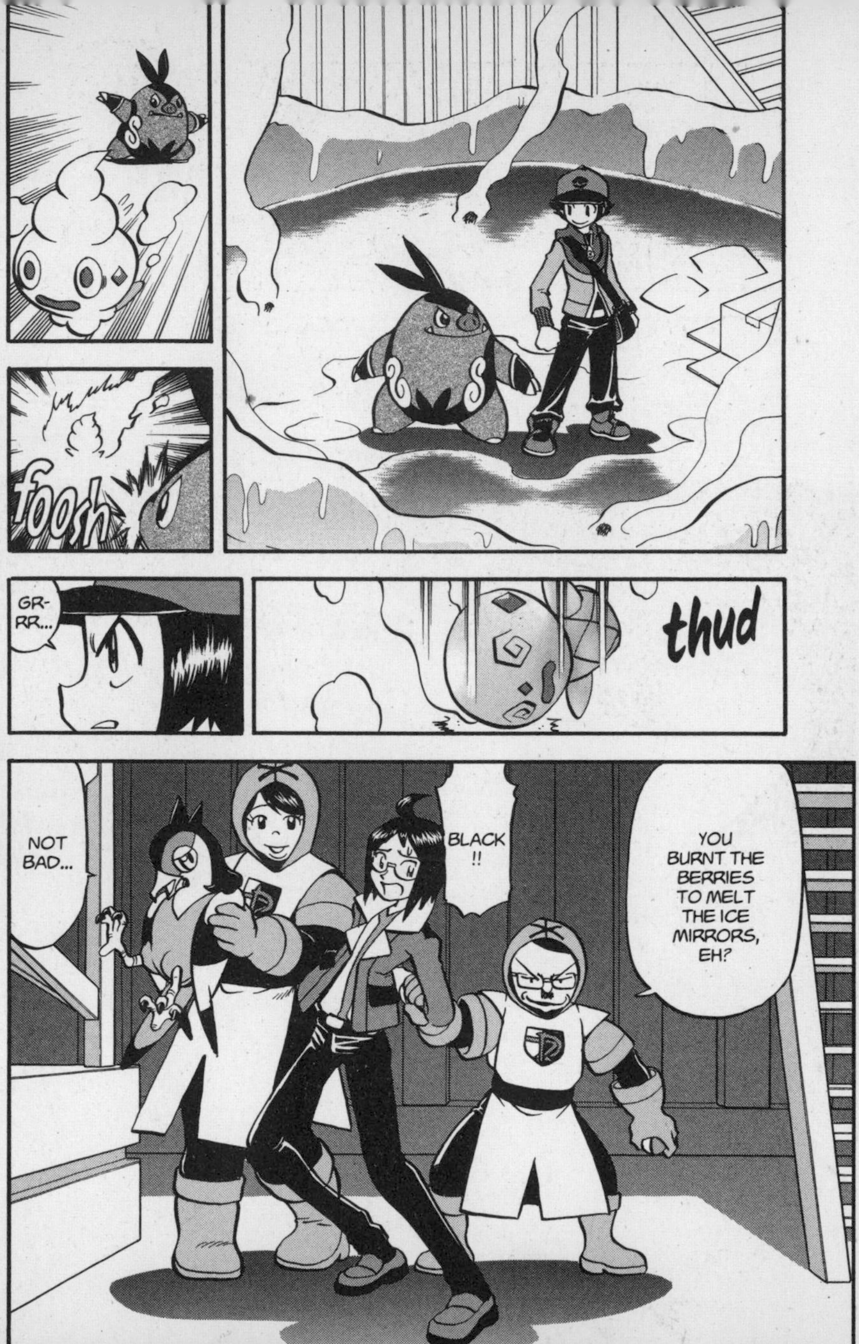
foosh
GR-RR...
thud
YOU BURNT THE BERRIES TO MELT THE ICE MIRRORS, EH?
BLACK !!
NOT BAD...

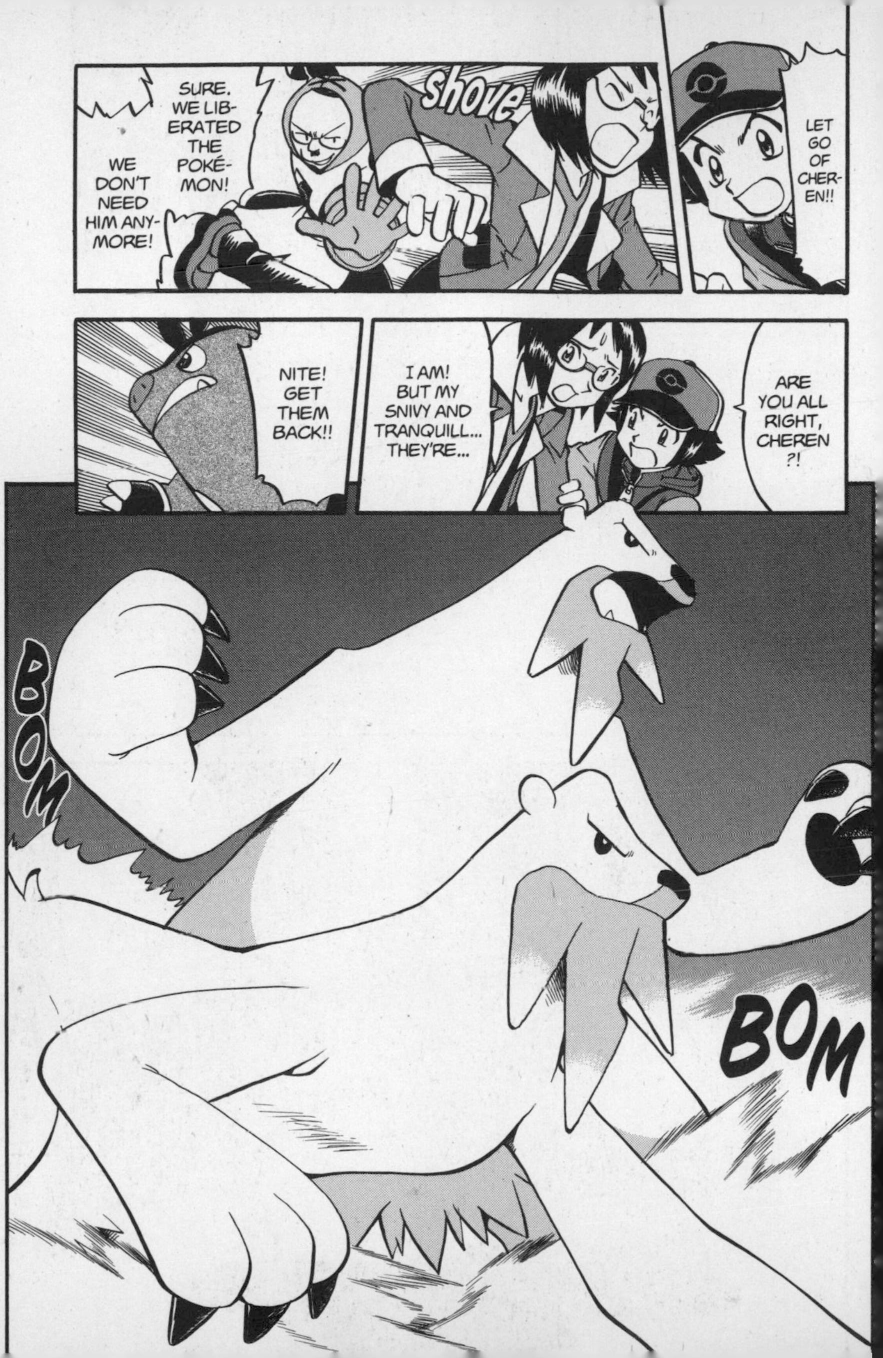
LET GO OF CHEREN!!
SURE. WE LIBERATED THE POKÉMON!
WE DON'T NEED HIM ANYMORE!
shove
ARE YOU ALL RIGHT, CHEREN?!
I AM! BUT MY SNIVY AND TRANQUILL... THEY'RE...
NITE! GET THEM BACK!!
BOM
BOM

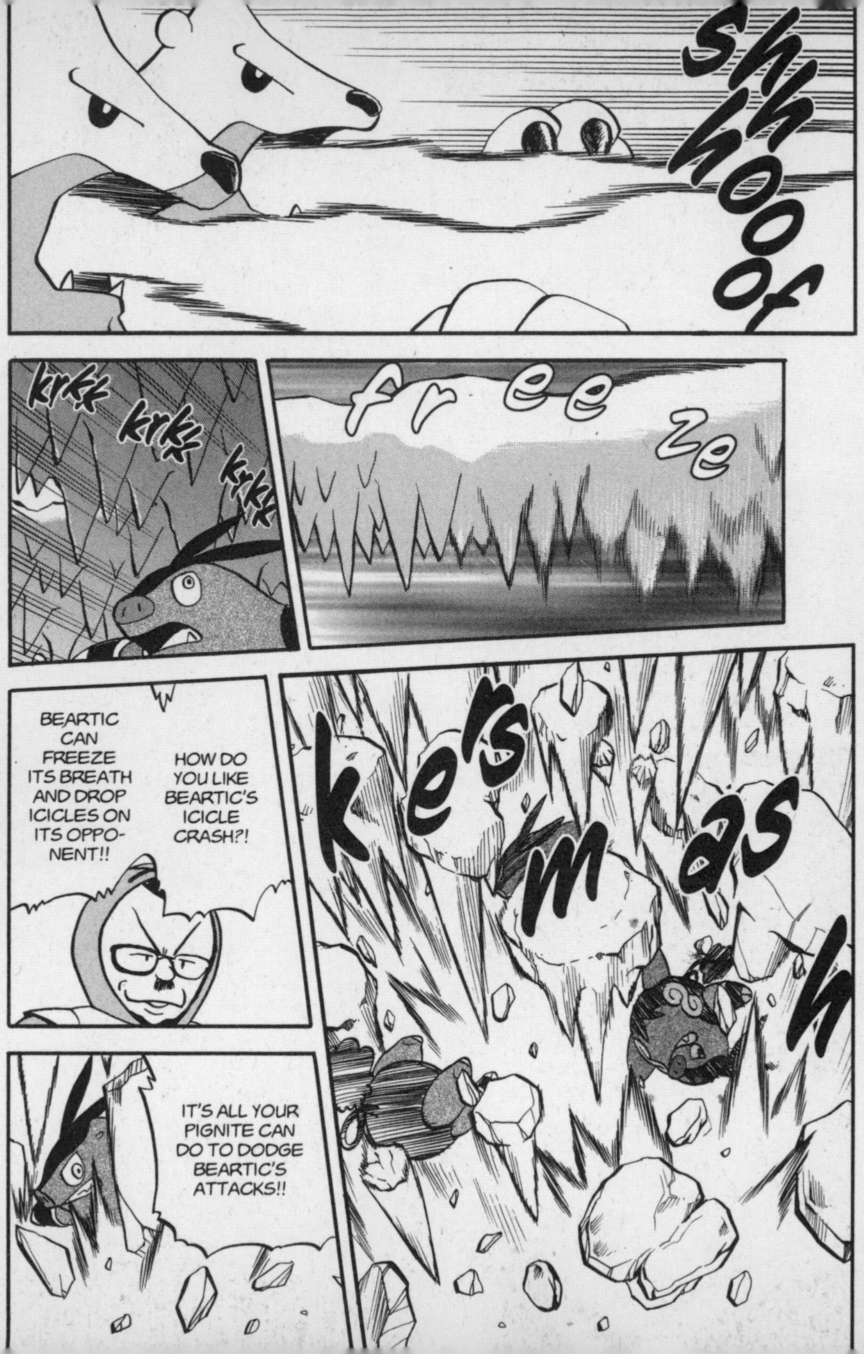

shhooof
krkk krkk krkk
freeze
BEARTIC CAN FREEZE ITS BREATH AND DROP ICICLES ON ITS OPPO-NENT!!
HOW DO YOU LIKE BEARTIC'S ICICLE CRASH?!
kersmash
IT'S ALL YOUR PIGNITE CAN DO TO DODGE BEARTIC'S ATTACKS!!

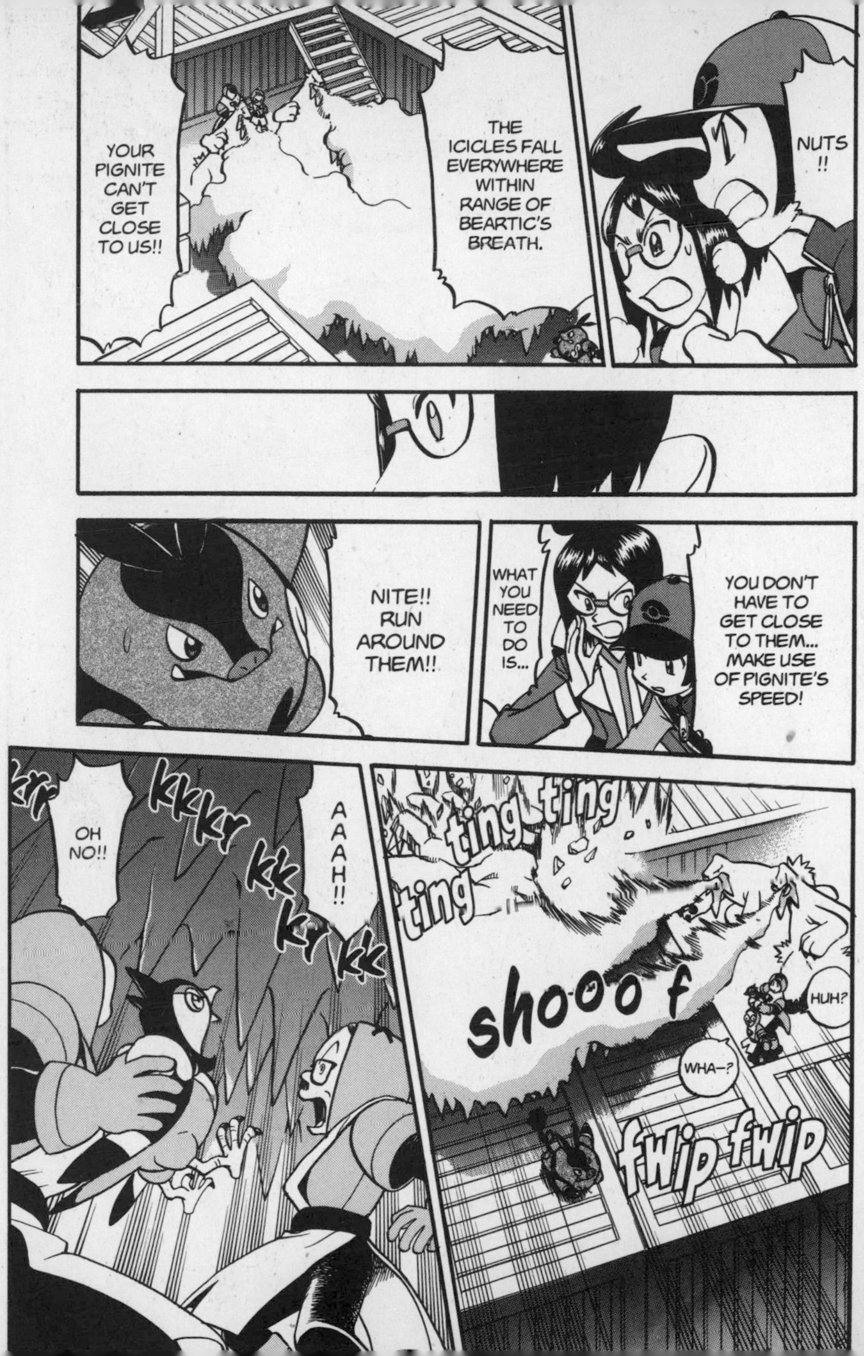
NUTS!!
THE ICICLES FALL EVERYWHERE WITHIN RANGE OF BEARTIC'S BREATH.
YOUR PIGNITE CAN'T GET CLOSE TO US!!
YOU DON'T HAVE TO GET CLOSE TO THEM... MAKE USE OF PIGNITE'S SPEED!
WHAT YOU NEED TO DO IS...
NITE!! RUN AROUND THEM!!
ting ting
ting
shooo f
HUH?
WHA--?
fwip fwip
AAAAH!!
kkkr
kk
kr
kk
OH NO!!

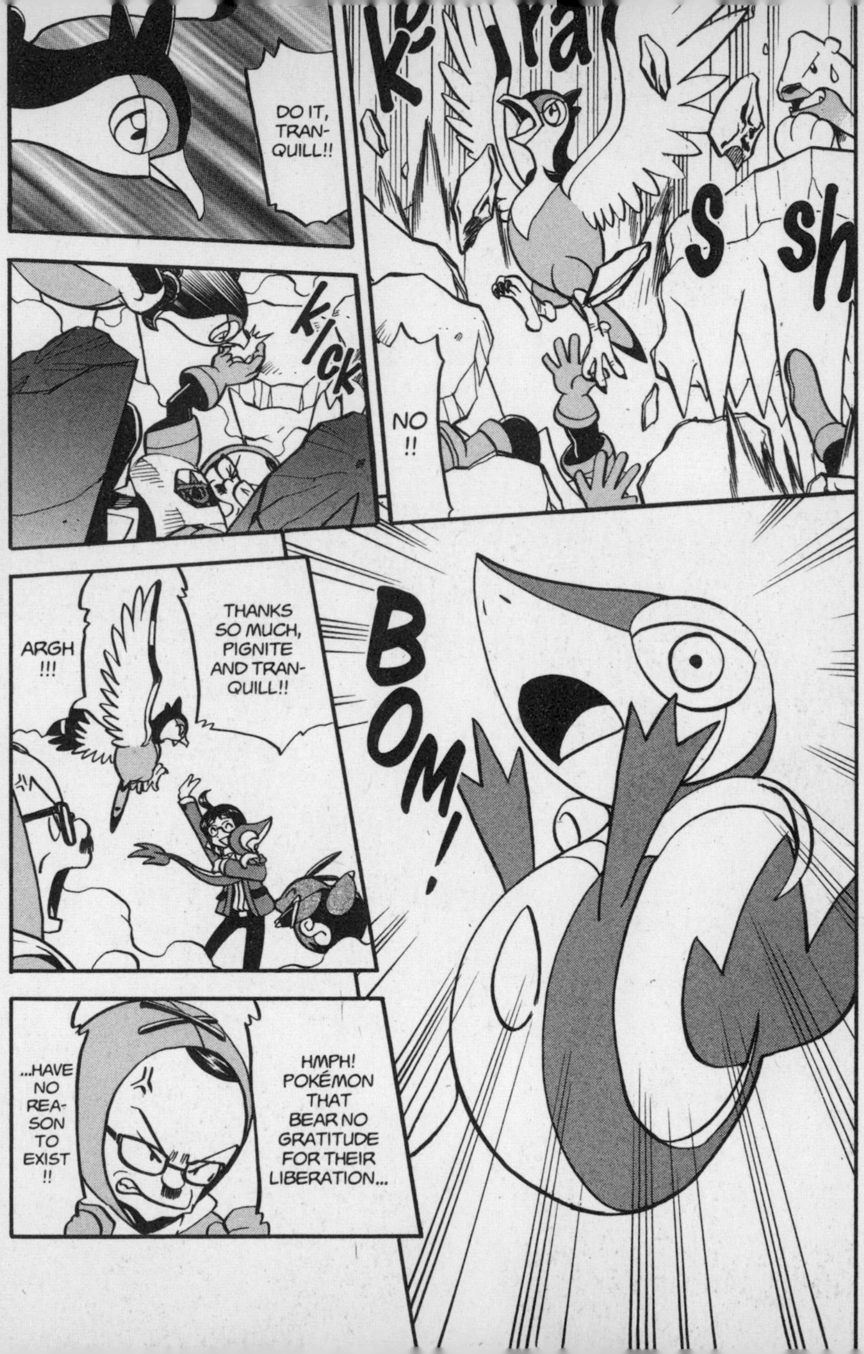
DO IT, TRAN-QUILL!!
KE... RA...
S SH...
KICK
NO !!
THANKS SO MUCH, PIGNITE AND TRAN-QUILL!!
ARGH !!!
BOOM!
HMPH! POKÉMON THAT BEAR NO GRATITUDE FOR THEIR LIBERATION...
...HAVE NO REA-SON TO EXIST !!

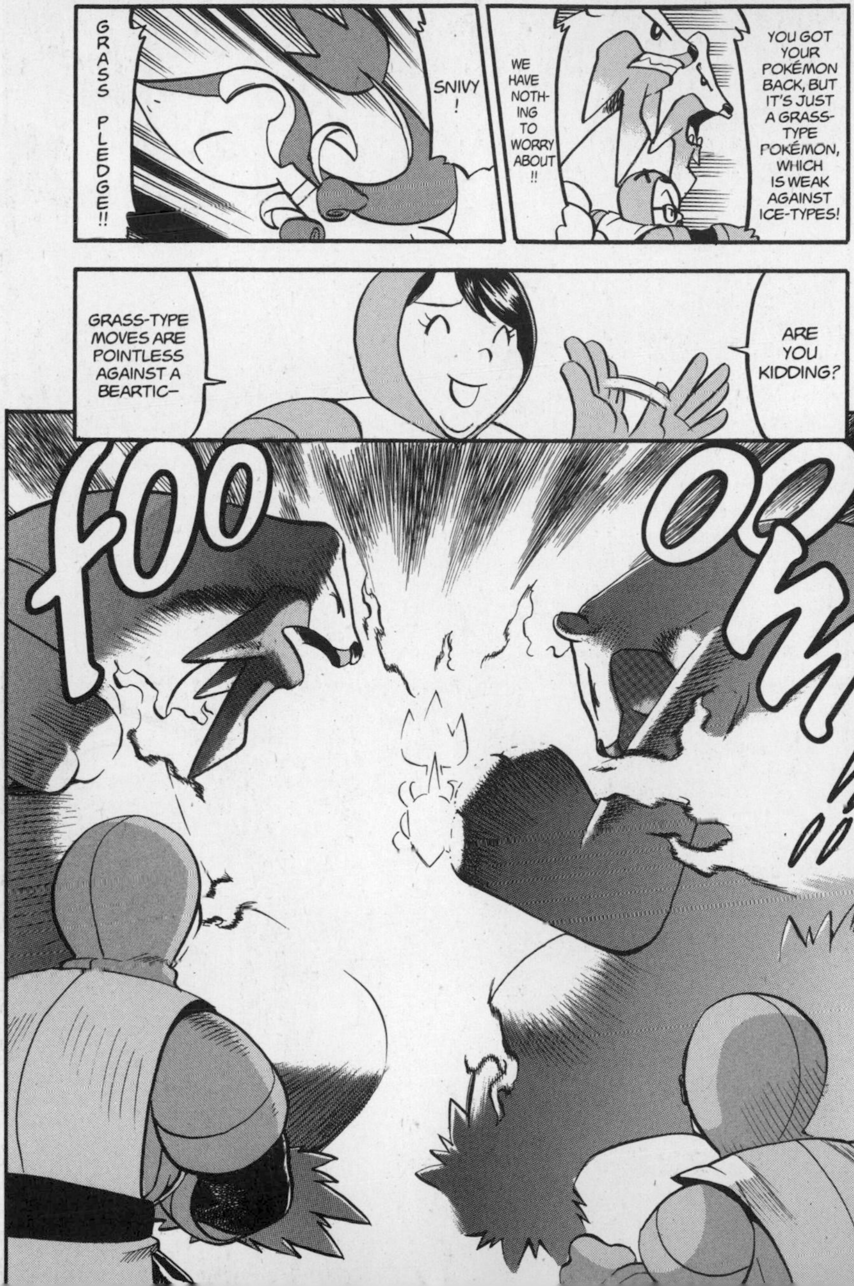
YOU GOT YOUR POKÉMON BACK, BUT IT'S JUST A GRASS-TYPE POKÉMON, WHICH IS WEAK AGAINST ICE-TYPES!
WE HAVE NOTHING TO WORRY ABOUT!!
SNIVY!
GRASS PLEDGE!!
ARE YOU KIDDING?
GRASS-TYPE MOVES ARE POINTLESS AGAINST A BEARTIC–
FOOOM!!

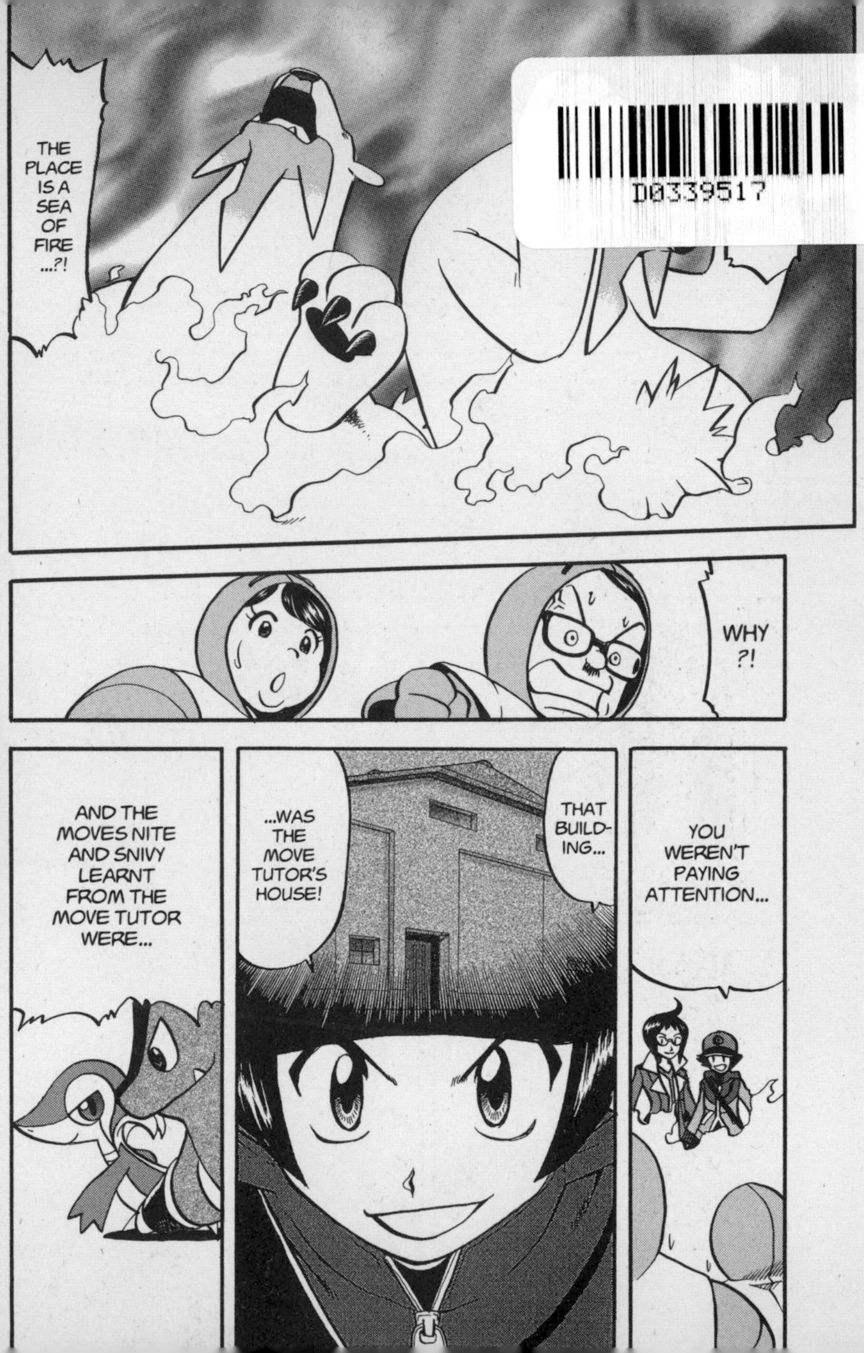
THE PLACE IS A SEA OF FIRE ...?!
WHY ?!
YOU WEREN'T PAYING ATTENTION...
THAT BUILDING...
...WAS THE MOVE TUTOR'S HOUSE!
AND THE MOVES NITE AND SNIVY LEARNT FROM THE MOVE TUTOR WERE...

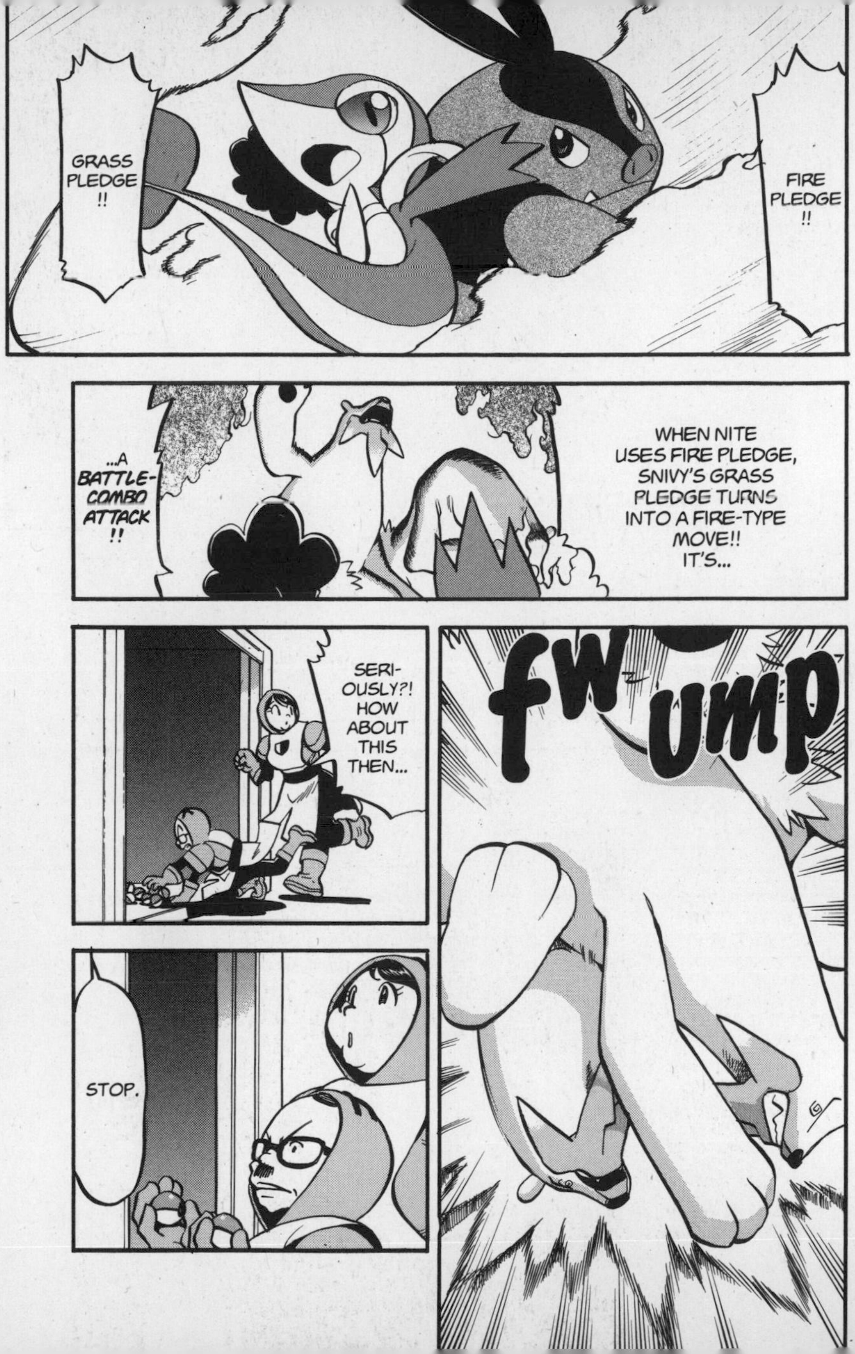
GRASS PLEDGE !!
FIRE PLEDGE !!
...A BATTLE-COMBO ATTACK !!
WHEN NITE USES FIRE PLEDGE, SNIVY'S GRASS PLEDGE TURNS INTO A FIRE-TYPE MOVE!! IT'S...
FWUMP
SERI-OUSLY?! HOW ABOUT THIS THEN...
STOP.

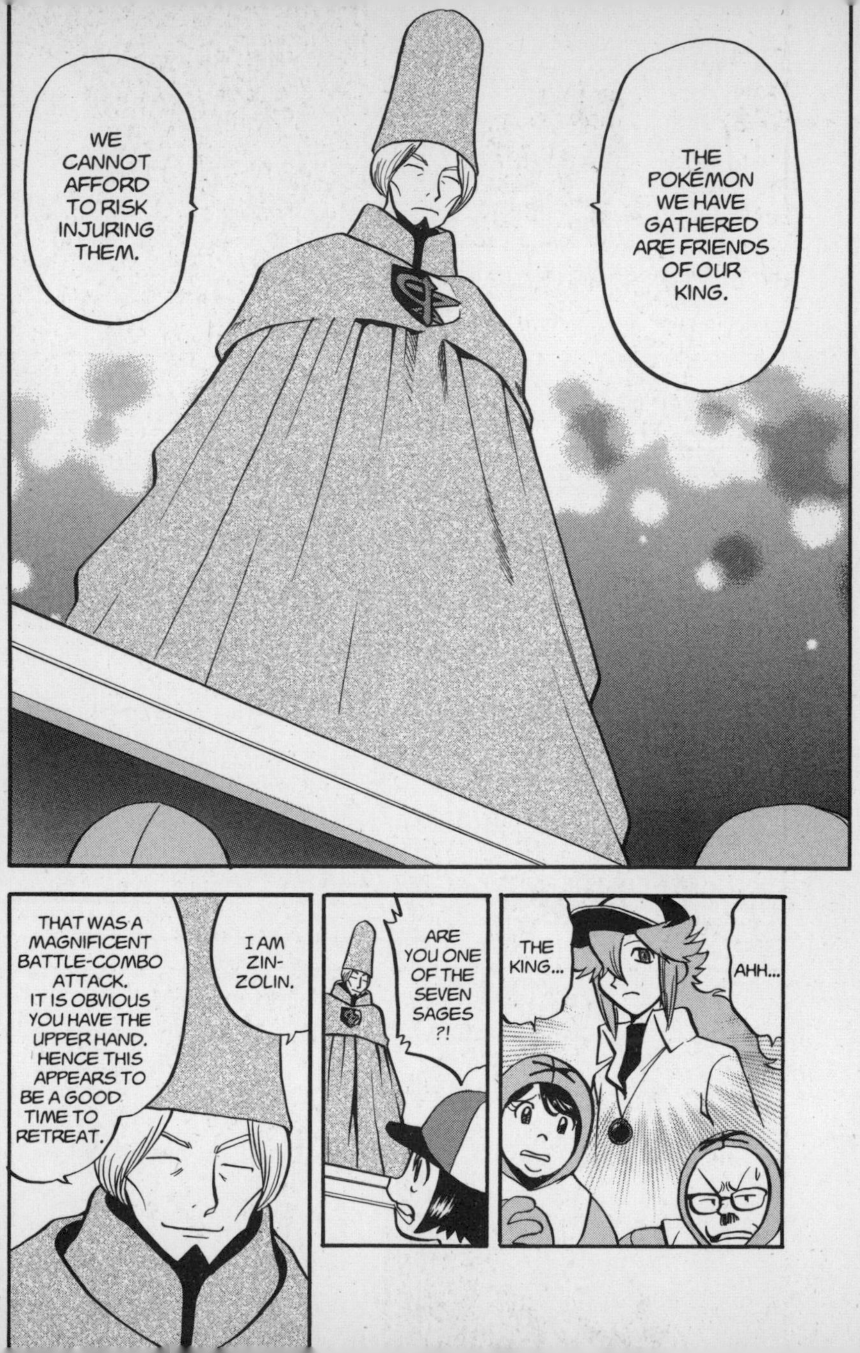
THE POKÉMON WE HAVE GATHERED ARE FRIENDS OF OUR KING.
WE CANNOT AFFORD TO RISK INJURING THEM.
AHH...
THE KING...
ARE YOU ONE OF THE SEVEN SAGES ?!
I AM ZIN-ZOLIN.
THAT WAS A MAGNIFICENT BATTLE-COMBO ATTACK. IT IS OBVIOUS YOU HAVE THE UPPER HAND. HENCE THIS APPEARS TO BE A GOOD TIME TO RETREAT.

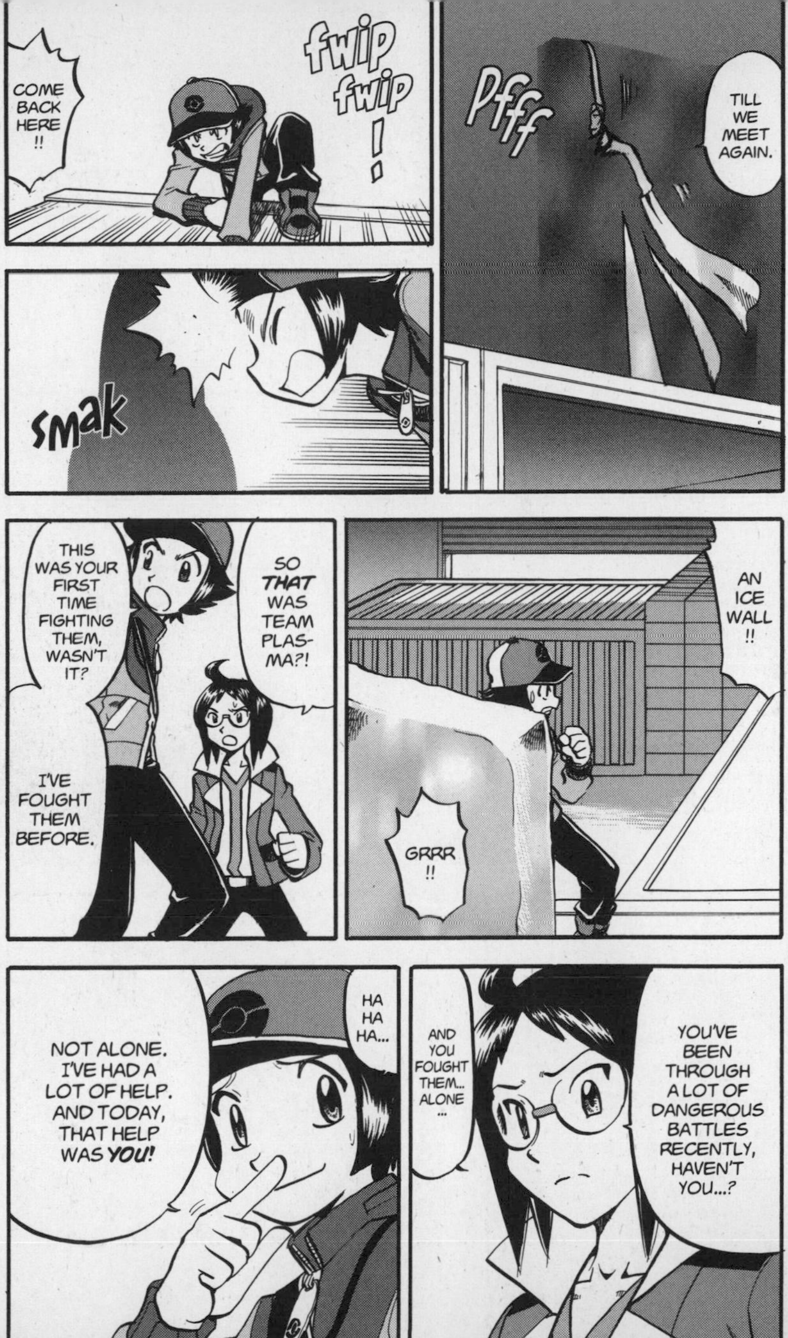
Pfff
TILL WE MEET AGAIN.
COME BACK HERE!!
fwip fwip!
SMAK
AN ICE WALL!!
GRRR!!
SO THAT WAS TEAM PLASMA?!
THIS WAS YOUR FIRST TIME FIGHTING THEM, WASN'T IT?
I'VE FOUGHT THEM BEFORE.
YOU'VE BEEN THROUGH A LOT OF DANGEROUS BATTLES RECENTLY, HAVEN'T YOU...?
AND YOU FOUGHT THEM... ALONE...
HA HA HA...
NOT ALONE. I'VE HAD A LOT OF HELP. AND TODAY, THAT HELP WAS YOU!

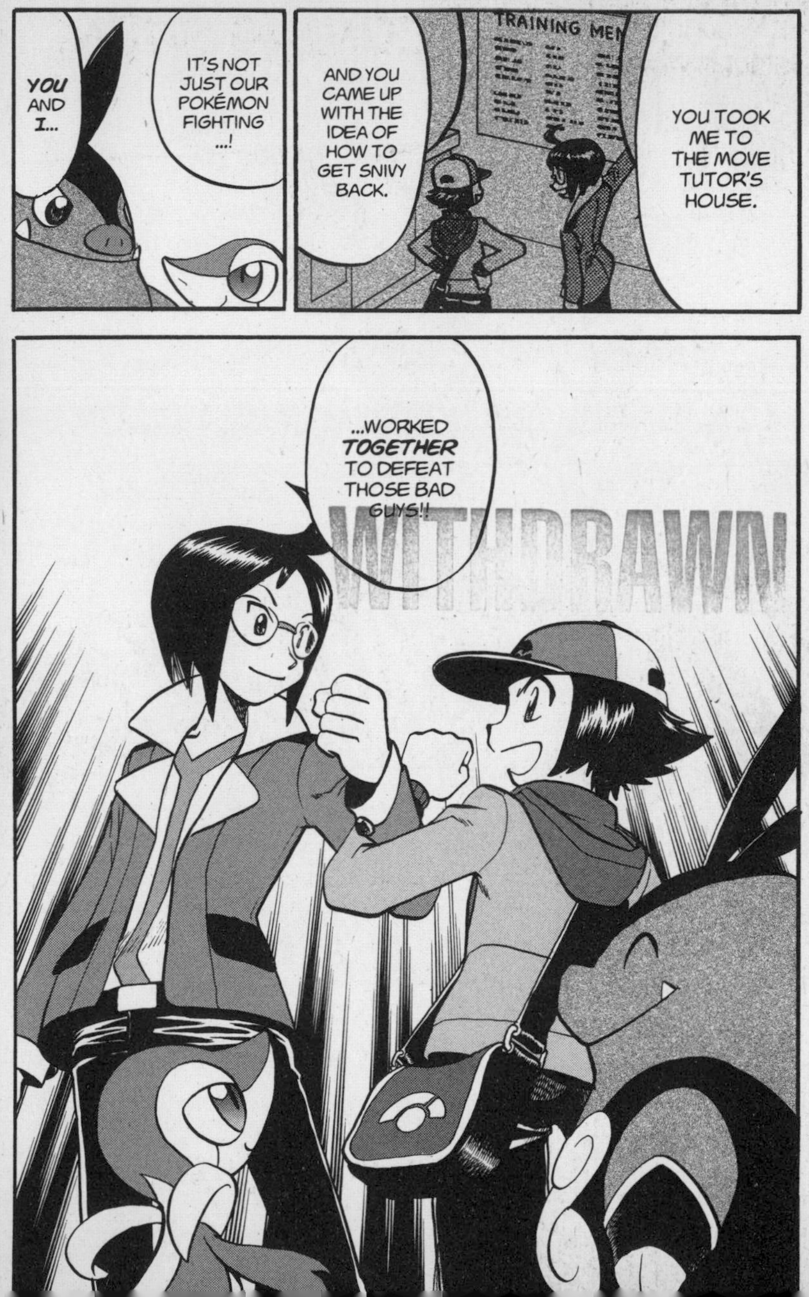
TRAINING MEN
YOU TOOK ME TO THE MOVE TUTOR'S HOUSE.
AND YOU CAME UP WITH THE IDEA OF HOW TO GET SNIVY BACK.
IT'S NOT JUST OUR POKÉMON FIGHTING ...!
YOU AND I...
...WORKED TOGETHER TO DEFEAT THOSE BAD GUYS!!